Michael Innes

LORD MULLION'S SECRET

HOUSE OF
STRATUS

This edition published in 2001 by House of Stratus, an imprint of
House of Stratus Ltd, Thirsk Industrial Park, York Road, Thirsk,
North Yorkshire, YO7 3BX, UK.
Also at: House of Stratus Inc., 2 Neptune Road, Poughkeepsie, NY 12601, USA.

www.houseofstratus.com

Typeset by House of Stratus, printed and bound by Short Run Press Limited.

A catalogue record for this book is available from the British Library
and the Library of Congress.

ISBN 1-84232-743-7

1

The Mullions were still quite comfortably off, although they no longer managed to pay their way in the entirely unobtrusive fashion they would have wished. Twice a week, and through the greater part of the year, they were obliged to turn Mullion Castle into a Stately Home. The disturbance was heralded shortly after breakfast, when Lord Mullion ascended to the leads and himself hoisted his personal standard above the battlements. He didn't greatly care for thus announcing to the world that he was 'in residence', since it seemed to him that whether he was at Mullion or not was a private matter with which the world had nothing to do. This particular small ostentation, indeed, was perfectly orthodox among his peers, a clear majority of whom probably maintained the habit. But Lord Mullion was a retiring man, who had to be kept up to the mark in the matter by his wife. 'Hang out our banners on the outward walls,' Lady Mullion would instruct him as she finished her second cup of coffee. 'The cry is still "They come".' And of course it was very desirable that they should come, since the reference was not to a hostile army but to the cars and char-a-bancs which would presently be bumping up the drive. So Lord Mullion did as he was told, consoling himself with the thought that his gesture could be construed as being, like Macbeth's, one of defiance rather than of welcome.

But Lord Mullion did on every occasion himself punctiliously welcome the small posse of gentlewomen – locally recruited and in reduced circumstances – upon whom he relied for the purpose of guiding visitors round the castle. It gratified tourists, he had been told, to entertain the vague belief that it was members of the Wyndowe family itself who were doing them this semi-menial service. Indeed, from time to time Lord Mullion afforded some solid ground for a persuasion of this sort by himself issuing entrance tickets at a small table placed beneath the portcullis. While thus occupied he quite readily forgot the mild indignity of the whole affair and welcomed his visitors with the same unaffected cordiality that he would have directed upon acquaintances of his own sort whom his wife had invited to luncheon. This duty performed, however, he would then retire with the rest of his household to what the shepherding ladies described as the 'private wing'. As Mullion Castle was not particularly large (except for the moat, which was enormous), and as most of what there was of it was well worth seeing, this meant rather a cooped-up existence for two days out of seven. But the money flowed in and was not to be quarrelled with.

On the whole it was only the servants who actively disapproved of being 'open' every Wednesday and Saturday. Like the family, they were kept out of sight, so there was no question of their picking up tips from the tourists, visitors, sightseers, or whatever the invading hordes were to be called. Even the teas on offer in the great tithe barn were served by respectable women from the two nearest villages, since Lady Mullion found this arrangement useful both as an engine of patronage and as a means of maintaining desirable friendly relations with that particular stratum of her neighbours. And the indoor staff did have a certain amount of extra work on the 'open' days. Strips of stout drugget had to be put down over valuable but perilously antique carpets, and various articles of furniture in similar condition had to be secured behind little rope barriers as in an old-fashioned picture gallery. Moreover there was a good deal of miscellaneous clearing up to do when the day's traffic was over.

Lady Mullion herself undertook one or two slightly vexatious tasks. She enjoyed deploying rather more in the way of floral arrangements than the household would normally have been content to accept (or the gardeners to supply). But the whole question of 'being lived in' was a tricky one. The char-a-banc people in particular

– the Mullions had been assured – liked to feel that in every room they visited a normal routine of the most aristocratic sort had been going on only minutes before. Lord Mullion thought there was a great deal of good sense in this. Nothing was more depressing, he was accustomed to say, than those châteaux on the Loire where, in the middle of gardens and waterways still admirably maintained, stands an enormous untenanted house with no more than a few sticks of tables and chairs and mouldering beds scattered at random here and there. But just where did one stop in the creating of this effect – or of this illusion, as it sometimes was? If one laid out preparations for bacon and eggs in a modest way in the breakfast room was it sensible to have a dinner-table awaiting almost innumerable banqueters on display at the other end of the castle? How lavishly, Lady Mullion asked herself, ought one to spread around those rather boring periodicals devoted to the celebration of fashionable life and rural pursuits? Again, what about Henry's cigars – so decidedly one among his few extravagances: ought the box to remain (open even) on his writing table in the library, or ought it to be shoved into a drawer? And then there were the photographs, family and other. The Mullions rather went in for these; they were perched in silver frames on little tables all over the place. Lord Mullion was a trifle vague about the several generations of Wyndowes thus on view, and only his wife could put a name to the army of relations, some in bath chairs and some in perambulators, thus patiently waiting to be recalled to mind. And there was the special case of the royal family. The Wyndowes happened to be among those of their kind who held the House of Windsor in high regard, and sundry exalted persons, sensible of the fact, had responded with the gracious bestowal of a signed photograph. Such exhibits meant much more to the majority of the 'patrons' (as Lord Mullion with a mild irony sometimes termed his customers) than did the portraits of even the most authentically Tudor Wyndowes. And there was something not quite agreeable about this.

The problem of the photographs was a little exacerbated by the particular method of showing the castle which had been chosen by

Lord Mullion. It had been explained to him by the experts in such enterprises that one can set about this in one of two ways. One can post, as it were, a sentinel or guard in every room and commanding every corridor, and allow one's visitors either to wander at will or to follow at their own pace a route marked out by a series of directing arrows pinned up in appropriate places. Or one can gather the visitors in clumps, and send the successive clumps round at convenient intervals under the wardenship of an individual guide. Lord Mullion had plumped for the latter method. He had already benevolently determined that the job should be in the hands of those elderly women of good family but narrow means (a number of them actually kinswomen of a remote sort) who abounded in the neighbourhood. They might not be terribly well informed, or even 'educated' in the modern sense, and therefore be a little uncertain as to which had been Oliver Cromwell and which Thomas. But essentially they were in the know, and their poise and self-confidence, let alone the perfect amenity of their address, would be far from faltering even were they caught out by some tedious person who had been mugging up from his guide-book. And it had seemed to Lord Mullion that it would be less demeaning were these ladies to take round groups in a companionable and conversable way than simply to stand guard here and there over the family spoons and forks. But this did involve their having to answer impertinent questions about the occupants of the perambulators and bath chairs, or even to opine whether it might be that Lord and Lady Mullion were among those privileged occasionally to 'stop by' at Buckingham Palace.

Of course nothing of all this really bothered the Mullions very much. They were confident people, amused rather than bewildered by the oddity of the times. What Lord Mullion called dismissively 'the current drift in social legislation' had to be admitted as variously vexatious. It could even be felt occasionally as lapping a little ominously against the walls of the castle, rather as if cannon balls were plopping into the moat. (Not that the moat could really be plopped into, since it was dry and a mass of daffodils.) But it would have taken a rumbling of the tumbrils across the inner ward of the castle itself to persuade these long-established persons that they were under any sort of threat. Having always shied away from anything other than landowning they were without any great fortune themselves. But a surprisingly high proportion of the total wealth of England belonged, if not to their friends, at least to people with whom it would be perfectly tolerable to sustain a nodding acquaintanceship. So it would be foolish to be flustered by the vagaries of one or another ephemeral political set-up. The char-a-bancs, like governments, came and went, while life in Mullion Castle and on its surrounding acres continued undisturbed.

The contents of the ancient dwellings were substantially undisturbed too. During recent generations its owners had been spacing out their demise at intervals long enough to be decidedly advantageous from a financial point of view, so that death duties had been coped with without any disastrous dispersal of goods, chattels, heirlooms and paraphernalia. Some notable possessions had until recently even been less disturbed than the lawyers and insurance people had been quite happy about. Thus for a very long time the three Nicholas Hilliard miniatures had simply hung on a moth-eaten velvet panel in the drawing-room, from which they could be lifted and handed round for admiration and comment after a dinner-party. But about these prudence had at length prevailed. They were now disposed in a showcase cunningly anchored to the floor, and beneath a sheet of some transparent substance guaranteed to resist a sledgehammer. There were, of course, numerous other objects of considerable value on view. But few of them could simply have been slipped into a pocket – and the guides, moreover, were well aware of what it was particularly desirable to keep an eye on. The only notable theft to date had been of a walking-stick much prized by Lord Mullion as having at one time been the property (he believed – but nobody knew why) of the first Duke of Wellington.

Shortly after the present chronicle opens, however, it was to be discovered that there had been a theft of a different character from Mullion Castle. On this occasion an object of considerable value was involved – and a great deal of perplexity as well.

2

Henry Wyndowe and Charles Honeybath had been schoolfellows, and now the first was a peer and the second a painter. Although painters (even Royal Academicians) are nothing like so grand as peers (or at least as peers of ancient creation), the two had remained more or less familiarly acquainted. Honeybath was the elder by several years, and as a consequence it had once been the future Lord Mullion's business to tidy his study, toast his crumpets, get the mud off his rugger boots, and accept a ritual admonitory swipe on the behind from time to time. Lord Mullion looked back on this feudal servitude as if it had been a warmly affectionate relationship, and Honeybath, as happens with fagmasters, had been quite fond of young Wyndowe in a casual fashion. So they continued to meet – and not merely as a matter of chance encounter – during several decades. The intimacy had not developed, however, as a family affair. Honeybath had become a widower after only a few years of marriage, and had grown rather fonder of his club than of other men's houses. He had never been a guest at Mullion Castle. Lord Mullion in fact knew more about Honeybath's pictures than Honeybath did about Lord Mullion's family. (The pictures, and particularly the portraits, were on annual display; the Wyndowes didn't much go in for public occasions.) Lord Mullion wasn't exactly a connoisseur. But he respected the arts in a general way, although his attention was inclined a little to wander when specific works of art were obtruded upon his notice – unless, indeed, dairy cattle or pedigree bulls were prominent in the composition. And even in a picture gallery

Honeybath always took pleasure in meeting his one-time fag. This even held when Lord Mullion one day turned up unheralded at his Chelsea studio.

The studio was no more than a studio, although a commodious one, and it was situated a couple of blocks away from Honeybath's flat. Honeybath liked this arrangement. He liked the sense of closing a front door behind him five times a week and setting off to work like any other normal citizen. Correspondingly, he liked leaving his work behind him at the end of the day. If your painting-room was across the corridor or up an attic staircase you were under the temptation to dodge into it at all hours and take a lick at this or a dab at that. It was a habit particularly easy to fall into if you were a man without domestic ties, and in Honeybath's experience good seldom came of it.

Yet there was one disadvantage about this disposition of things. When you work, for the most part alone, in an isolated studio you are more vulnerable than in a dwelling with a household around you. There is nobody to say you are out, and you either have to receive casual callers with what civility you can muster or be suspected of ungraciously skulking in a cupboard until your importunate visitor has taken himself (or more probably herself) off again. And such people can he not only importunate but occasionally impertinent as well – behaving as if in a picture shop and poking around all over the place. It was even possible to suspect some of them as seeking evidences of what used to he called Bohemian life. But Lord Mullion was not in any category of this sort, so that Honeybath's welcome was unforced and immediate.

'My dear Henry,' he said, 'how delightful to see you!'

'Can I come in, Charles? Is it perfectly convenient? I mean, are you painting somebody – one of the nobs, as it regularly seems to be nowadays?'

'Nothing of the kind. I'm simply messing around. So hang up your hat. And you're a nob yourself, aren't you? Only nobs have hats any longer. Do you remember, Henry, the absurd things we had to wear even to walk down that High Street? All gone, I'm told.'

Honeybath and Lord Mullion had been 'Charles' and 'Henry' to one another ever since Honeybath's last year at school, when they had found themselves by chance sentenced to improve their acquaintance with the French language and French manners throughout the Easter holidays in the same horrible French family. Only on returning to school they had become for a time 'Honeybath' and 'Wyndowe' again in deference to the moral code operative in the period. But Christian names had returned quite naturally after that.

'As a matter of fact,' Lord Mullion said, glancing round him, 'this is a familiar set-up to me at the moment. I've been sitting to a chap not a mile away. Is "sitting" right? He did me standing, as it happens. It made me feel so much like my own butler that I expect to have a thoroughly butler-like appearance in the finished portrait. Fair enough. The Wyndowes started off as butlers, as everybody knows.'

'Probably quite some time ago.'

'Well, not really. Round about 1580, say. But the trouble has been that they've regularly had themselves painted or limned or whatever they called it ever since, and, my children got together and said my turn had come. And standing up seemed to be the traditional thing. Holding a sword or a hunting-crop or a six-foot walking stick, or pointing out an order of battle on a map. Actually, remaining on my two feet was something of an advantage, since I was able just to take a turn around the place when I had a prompting that way. The painter didn't seem to mind. He's a nice chap – although no genius, if you ask me.'

'Not many of us are that, Henry. But you never know how posterity may judge. Can't you hear somebody saying, "They've sent a decent little Dutchman to take my likeness. Name of Rubens, or some such. No reason to suppose he can paint for toffee. But a useful man, I'm told, to send on a confidential mission"?' Honeybath was hospitably producing drinks as he offered this whimsical travesty of art-history. 'Will you take a glass of madeira?'

'Yes, indeed. The truth is, Charles, that I've come on a confidential mission myself. Or not exactly a mission, since nobody has sent me and it's all my own idea.' Lord Mullion paused – seemingly to take a sniff at the madeira, but actually (Honeybath discerned) because of some uncharacteristic embarrassment. This, indeed, wasn't difficult to elucidate. It troubled Lord Mullion that the commission he had just described hadn't been offered to his old schoolfellow. And now – this was clear too – he had some delicate point to make. 'I'm wondering, you see' – he resumed, taking a plunge – 'whether you'd consider painting Mary. For the other side of the fireplace, so to speak. She's a damned sight better worth painting than I am, and a tiptop painter ought to be rounded up to do the job. Would you consider it, Charles, my dear fellow?'

So here, suddenly, was a tricky situation – but of a kind with which Honeybath was by no means unacquainted. Painting the portrait of an old chum is usually plain sailing. You simply go straight ahead, and within half-a-dozen sittings you are revealing what you have never noticed in forty years: the ape or poodle or clown or saloon-bar type that lies at scratching distance beneath that familiar mug. But the old chum knows what he has booked in for, and is delighted (even to the pitch of roaring with laughter rather than rage) when what you have made of him is revealed to his astonished gaze. For the entire candour of schoolboys, of undergraduates, is between you still, and carries the day. But an old chum's wife is a different matter, and you may find yourself in the end faced with a polite but angry couple. What you have put on your canvas isn't what the woman sees in her looking-glass and has taught her husband to see. The woman may know her 'weak points' even to excess, and be coldly candid about them when having her clothes cut and her hair dressed. But all this is mere aesthetics. And portrait-painting is about something more and other than how near, or remote from, winning a beauty contest your subject happens to be. In fact portrait-painting, like major surgery, ought not to be undertaken by a family friend.

Of course Honeybath, as has been explained, was scarcely that so far as the Mullions were concerned. He had done no more than meet Lady Mullion three or four times on essentially public occasions. And what he could recall of her now was reassuring. She was a handsome woman, and one who hadn't flinched from letting what of good and ill had come to her stamp itself on her face. Honeybath knew he would enjoy painting Lady Mullion. This didn't necessarily mean that he would make a success of the job. But it was a favourable omen, all the same.

'But of course I'll consider it!' he said. 'I'm very, very pleased, Henry, that you should propose the idea.'

'I know that you must be tremendously busy, Charles.' Lord Mullion was clearly delighted, and spoke as if a burden of guilt had been lifted from his shoulders. 'You'll understand, I'm sure, that the other affair was arranged by the young people entirely above my head. But if I can have Mary by you – '

'As you certainly shall. It's true it will take a little fitting in, but it will be at the cost of no more than a few harmless fibs. How long are you both staying in town?' Honeybath was well accustomed to having the exigencies of 'the Season' (followed by the necessity of shooting grouse) obtruded upon the craft of portraiture.

'In town?' There was simple surprise in Lord Mullion's repetition of the phrase. 'My dear man, I'm up only for the night myself. And Mary no longer comes near the place. She can't stick London, and I'm bound to say I sympathize with her. We're very quiet folk, you know – very quiet folk, indeed. Except on Wednesdays and Saturdays, that is – but I'll tell you about that later. You must come down and stay with us at Mullion, of course, and get a bit of country air, and tackle the assignment in your spare time and the occasional wet day.' Lord Mullion chuckled happily, well aware that this derogatory manner of speaking of the 'assignment' couldn't be taken as other than a joke. 'Dash it all, you've owed us a long visit for a long time.'

This last remark might perhaps have been described as a little lordly, since Honeybath (as has been recorded) had never been to Mullion Castle in his life. But here again was old-chum fun, and Honeybath didn't see how it was to be resisted. Accepting commissions on, as it were, a residential basis was something he had learnt to be chary of. It had got him into trouble before, and was basically unsound. It meant your becoming, in a restricted sense, a kind of court painter. You sketched the children, and even the dogs.

You had to take a fancy to this and that nook and corner of house and gardens and park, and delight yourself in consequence with little topographical tasks. It could be entirely enjoyable, and probably at Mullion it would be. Still, Honeybath's studio was where Honeybath liked to work.

Lord Mullion sensed this hesitation, and had the guile (an immemorial inherited guile) to begin making anxious alternative suggestions at once. The Mullions themselves no longer had a town house, or even a town chicken-coop. But their son already kept a pad (odd term, eh?) in Kensington, and something could certainly be fixed up. Honeybath, aware that he had been on the verge of graceless behaviour, hastened to express his pleasure at the prospect of being a guest at the castle. He even remembered the Hilliards, which were famous, and said how much he looked forward to being shown those minute masterpieces. Presumably – although he couldn't remember – they were portraits of early Wyndowes. He did remember that Hilliard had engraved Queen Elizabeth's second great seal in 1586– a fact suggesting that Henry's family must have prospered in the buttling line with notable rapidity.

It was of his family – but of his family as at present constituted – that Lord Mullion now began to speak.

'There are a great many Wyndowes around,' he said, 'and most of them in what you might call obscure circumstances. Not in indigence or gaol or anything embarrassing of that kind. But in the colonies or in business: that sort of thing.' Lord Mullion paused on this; it was frequently apparent that he enjoyed indulging in mild humour. 'You don't often find them in the news. But there they are, beavering away at this and that with the greatest devotion. A lot of them turn up on us from time to time, and it's not a thing to take exception to. The head of a family can't ignore an occasional nod from a kinsman, or even deny him a square meal when it appears to be called for. Still, there are undeniably the devil of a lot of Wyndowes. A kind of Crystal Palace of them, in fact.' This was clearly a familiar witticism. 'Fortunately Mary is uncommonly good at keeping tabs on them. She has one of those little card-index things, and can do you the gen on anybody who calls cousins in two ticks.'

'That must be very useful.' Honeybath felt he had been innocently required to admire this blending of a modish with an archaic vocabulary. 'But what about your immediate household, Henry?'

'Ah, that's not complicated at all, I'm glad to say. Everybody quite tolerably pleased with everybody else, for one thing – which is not a particularly fashionable state of affairs in families nowadays, I'm told. Applies even to Camilla.'

'Camilla?'

'Great-aunt Camilla, you know. At least that's what we call her, although of course she can't be the great-aunt of everybody around the place. She's the niece of my Wyndowe grandfather – so I have to regard her as a close relation, and there she is. At Mullion, I mean – and has been for a long time. Never married, and that's no doubt what made her a bit difficult in middle life. But since going out of her mind she's been no trouble in the world. Or only now and then.' Lord Mullion accepted a second glass of madeira. 'There's a streak of oddity in us that shows up every now and then. Not one of those predictable things that regularly skips a generation or a couple of generations, like earthquakes and volcanic eruptions and so forth. Whether it's advantageous to have that sort of advance notice of such troubles it's hard to say. My own children are sane enough, and commonly thought to take after their mother. I think you'll like them.'

'I'm sure I shall. Are they mostly at home still?'

'The girls seem content to spend most of their holidays with us – and Cyprian most of his vacations, for that matter. Cyprian's a Kingsman now, I'm glad to say, and enjoying Cambridge very much. Doing very well, too, in some boat or other. He went in for wet bobbing at the start, of course. Wasn't our line – eh, Charles?'

'No more it was.'

'I could never understand the desire to be a galley-slave. Much better to do something you can let up on when you want to.' Lord

Mullion appeared to seek for an exemplification. 'Painting, for instance. Eh, Charles?'

'I've known painting to turn a little compulsive at times. And some of its swells are on record as having been quite unable to stop.'

'Amateurs, too, come to think of it.' Lord Mullion, who seemed to have time on his hands, had settled back contentedly in a shabby but commodious armchair. It struck Honeybath that he was, in fact, the very type of the perfectly contented man: one whose demands upon life had been modest and had seldom failed of fulfilment. 'You'll remember, Charles, that when we were small boys watercolour sketching still headed embroidering, and thumping the piano and the like, with the elderly idle women. I've known country houses plastered with the labours of female relatives from floor to ceiling. And Camilla had the mania in her time. We have stacks of her stuff stowed away at Mullion, and a few specimens tactfully on view as well. They may interest you.'

Honeybath, who (mistakenly, as it was to turn out) judged this improbable, asked a few questions about the interests and pursuits of Lady Mullion and her children. He heard without surprise that Lady Mullion was a devoted gardener. So was her elder daughter, Patty. Patty, indeed, was rapidly overtaking her mother in command of the more esoteric aspects of this appropriate pursuit. Boosie, the younger girl, had chosen on the other hand to take a precocious interest in politics, a sphere of activity to which singularly few Wyndowes had been notably drawn for some centuries. Boosie (it was a traditional family name, Lord Mullion explained) had successfully politicized the boarding-school of which she was now head girl, with the result that its ponies and lacrosse-sticks were at a discount, and ideological confrontations all the go. Of Cyprian, the future earl, it couldn't be said that he would ever be likely thus to move men. When he had done with all that strenuous ploughing up and down the Cam he would undoubtedly have to be 'got into something'. His father, it was true, had never very strikingly got out of Mullion Castle. But times were changing, and Cyprian would have to be found what Lord

13

Mullion frankly expressed as 'a niche with a good screw to it'. Cyprian – Lord Mullion reported with satisfaction – said that he was all for a good screw.

'And that's the lot,' Lord Mullion said. 'Except, of course, that there are a few other Wyndowes within a bow-shot or two. My brother Sylvanus, for example. Sylvanus has the dower house – naturally on the understanding that he clears out if and when Mary lines up for it. Sylvanus is much younger than I am, but at a bit of a loose end. They kicked him out of the army.'

'I'm sorry to hear it.' Honeybath felt that this ought to be said soberly.

'No, no – nothing of that kind.' Lord Mullion was amused. 'It was simply that Sylvanus isn't at all bright, and so they plucked him. He was quite frank about it. Nowadays the army is exams all the way up, and if you fail them they give you a nod and a wink, and that's that. Changed times again. It didn't help the poor devil a bit that he was Major the Honourable Sylvanus Wyndowe. Rather the opposite. Thought to be cumbrous, perhaps. However, he's fortunately given to what you might call rural pursuits. Proper in a Sylvanus, eh? Another old family name, of course. Camilla's father, another second son, was a Sylvanus. And so was mine.'

'Your father was a second son?' It didn't occur to Honeybath to dissimulate the fact that he was not well informed about Lord Mullion's ancestry.

'Good Lord, yes. My uncle Rupert would have succeeded, you know. But he died quite young and unmarried, so it was my father who came in. That's why I was Lord Wyndowe as a kid.'

'Which is what Cyprian is now.'

'Yes. Rather dull, he thinks it. But there isn't a handy second title around. Viscount Tom-noddy, or whatever. Rum things, titles of honour, and tiresome in shops. When I say "Lord Mullion" to a fellow I'm giving an order to he suspects me of being a con man at once.'

On this improbable note Lord Mullion got to his feet and took his leave, remarking that he would write about the details of 'their little plan' in a few days' time. It seemed probable to Honeybath that Henry's wife as yet knew nothing about it. Perhaps Henry was plotting a birthday present, and perhaps Lady Mullion wouldn't be too keen on the boring business of sitting for her portrait. But her husband gave no hint of this, and at the door of the studio he did get one detail clear.

'I'm told,' he said briskly, 'that two thousand guineas is the going rate.'

'Yes, it is.'

'Capital, Charles, my dear fellow.' Lord Mullion, already half in the open air, paused and chuckled cheerfully. 'Gad!' he said. 'It must be marvellous to coin money at that rate. Particularly, mark you, when richly deserved. Do you know? I can't be said ever to have earned a penny in my life – or not since you used to tip me half-a-crown for extra chores, eh? We'll look forward tremendously to your coming down.' And with this Lord Mullion waved his hat and walked away.

Left to himself, Charles Honeybath consulted his desk diary. It showed a good many portrait commissions lined up, and several of them would involve him with a man or woman who had booked his services – for that was what it came to – virtually on a postcard or over the telephone, and this after no more than a casual reconnaissance in a club or over a luncheon table. It was like whoredom, he told himself, this endless intimate clinching with total strangers. Or at least it was like this when one was feeling bad. When one was feeling good it was like something quite as exhausting and at the same time more difficult to define. In essence, perhaps, having an easel between you and a human being was no different from having it between you and a landscape. It was the same exploring and unveiling job. But at least a landscape didn't talk, or take irrational likings or dislikings to you. How pleasant to have been Corot, or one of those innumerable landscapists of the past who had their compositions unobtrusively peopled by figure-painters fetched in for the job.

This was a well-trodden little path in Honeybath's thought processes, and it didn't really mean much. He was in fact devoted to the region into which his bent and talents had taken him. And he found himself quite looking forward to the assignment which young Henry Wyndowe (now not so young Lord Mullion) was fixing up.

3

Lady Patience Wyndowe – 'Patty' in the family – nowadays frequently found herself wondering how Swithin Gore had come by his not very common Christian name. His father, she had gathered, had been Ammon Gore. 'Ammon', although not very common either, had apparently at one time enjoyed a certain rustic currency, whereas the only other Swithin she had ever come across was in a novel. The fictitious Swithin hadn't been a gardener's boy (which was the real Swithin's condition) but he had belonged roughly to that class of society – although there had been, at the same time, some gentle component to him the explanation of which now escaped Patty's memory. Sometimes it was possible to feel that a similar suggestion attached to Swithin Gore. The suggestion chiefly connected up with the way he looked at her when receiving this or that horticultural instruction. Swithin (who wasn't really a boy, and must indeed be within a year or two of her own age) owned a very direct glance. It wasn't impudent, or in any manner bold in the slightest degree. But it *was* direct, and at the same time distinguishably wondering. Wondering rather than admiring – and this had the happy effect of rendering it wholly unembarrassing. Patty felt that she was getting to know Swithin, with whom she had much to do, quite well. At least enough to realize, for instance, that he was an intelligent young man. It wasn't, however, well enough to ask him about his name. Or at least so Patty thought until she suddenly found that she was doing so.

'Swithin,' she said, 'what made them call you Swithin?'

Swithin straightened up – rather fast – from the flower bed over which he had been bending. Physically, Swithin was undeniably attractive. He was this all over. Even in the posture he had just abandoned, and when thus viewed from behind, this held of him – although its normal association for Patty would have been with vulgar postcards glimpsed at the seaside. But now Swithin was facing her, and he looked very well indeed.

'The 15th of July,' Swithin said, a shade shortly. 'My birthday.' And he added, after the slightest pause, 'M'lady.'

'Yes, of course. How stupid of me.' Patty wasn't going to show that she had been justly snubbed. And it *had* been stupid of her. Because of what it tells of the coming weather, St Swithin's Day is a landmark in the English rural mind, and it had been natural and even edifying for Ammon Gore to call his infant after the saint. It had been like naming as Noel a boy born at Christmas. And now, having been a little venturesome with her assistant, Patty went further. 'So how old are you now, Swithin?'

'Twenty. Did you say six inches?' This question, briskly uttered, referred to the dibbling operation in progress at the moment.

'Yes, I think so. And not too deep. We're not in a turnip field.'

'It would be a queer way to behave with turnips,' Swithin said matter-of-factly, and bent again to his task. He performed it from the waist and without bending his knees. This, muscularly, was the economical and professional thing. And, again, it was attractive in itself. 'How old are *you*?' Swithin asked, his nose close to the ground.

The comeback was unexpected, and Patty found it disconcerting as well. Or rather she found disconcerting the fact that her spontaneous reaction to Swithin's echoing her own question had been, if ever so faintly, disapproving. If she asked a young man his age why on earth shouldn't he ask her hers? Her father, she knew, would judge the garden boy's reciprocal curiosity to be entirely civilized and in order. Indeed, Swithin's tossing the ball briskly back had been much nicer in him than that snubby 'M'lady' he had started off with.

'Twenty-one,' she said, suddenly pleased and laughing. 'So we're both getting on. Do you like it here, Swithin?'

'I've been here always, haven't I?' Erect again, Swithin Gore made this reply with what appeared to be no enigmatical intention. But was that very straight glance faintly mocking as well? Lady Patience Wyndowe found herself, for reasons that were obscure to her, rather hoping that it was.

'Yes, I suppose you have,' she said. 'And I have too – except for going away to school. I didn't much care for that.'

'But Lady Lucy does.' Lady Lucy was Patty's younger sister Boosie. 'She has told me about some high old times.'

'Has she, now?' Patty was astonished by this information – and abruptly jealous of Boosie, whom she wouldn't have supposed ever to have held any conversation with Swithin at all. Perhaps Boosie was planning to convert Swithin to Euro-communism, or whatever it was that she at present believed in. 'My sister bosses her school, Swithin, and that's why she enjoys it. Did you boss yours?'

'Yes, I did.'

This had flashed out from Swithin in a surprising way. Patty had only a vague notion of the kind of school a garden boy came from, but supposed it to begin with toddlers in snot-covered smocks and end up with beefy louts and larking hoydens largely beyond anybody's control. The mere fact that he was alert and clever must have made Swithin something of an odd boy out. If he had really come out on top it was necessary to conclude that he had something. And this was becoming Patty's impression anyway.

But Swithin had returned to his work on the biennials, planting out with mathematical precision the wallflowers and polyanthus that would fill this one large bed in one of the several small gardens lying outside the moat of Mullion Castle. Patty was just deciding that it would be judicious (after this curious breakthrough) to leave him to it when Swithin spoke again.

'The poor man's flower,' Swithin said.

'What's that, Swithin?'

'The polyanthus. It's in a poem as that. "Or polyanthus, edged with golden wire, the poor man's flower." It's just like that, isn't it?'

'Yes – and how very interesting.' What Patty meant was that Swithin was very interesting. He was becoming rather alarming as well.

'Or did you ever hear,' Swithin asked, 'of something being described as smart as a gardener's dog with a polyanthus in his mouth?'

'I don't think I ever did.'

'Then you ought to have, m'lady. Because, you see, it's in *The Water-Babies*. And it must have been in your nursery, I'd be thinking, that book.'

'I suppose so. In fact, I'm sure it was.' Patty found herself not resenting the measure of reproof in Swithin's observation. She had also become conscious that Swithin, although he didn't talk in the refined manner of, say, Savine, her father's butler, didn't quite have the accents of a gardener's boy either. It was odd that her ear had never detected this now perfectly patent fact. As ears go, Swithin's must be better than hers. And he must have employed it, whether consciously or not, during such opportunities as he had of listening to the conversation of what Great-aunt Camilla would call his betters. Perhaps he had notions of improving himself, which would be sensible enough. More probably – since the result was so far from disagreeable – it was something that had just happened. But now a new line of inquiry had presented itself. And Patty, being a straightforward young woman, went ahead with it. 'Do you read a lot?' she asked.

'Yes.' This was the rather abrupt Swithin again. Patty recalled how the Vicar of Mullion, an old man given to antique usages, sometimes described himself as having been 'villaging' – by which he meant going round the cottagers and chatting them up. It wouldn't do to turn on a villaging act with this twenty-year-old young man. On the other hand, having once taken him on, as now, not as a hind but as a human being, why funk it? Patty again went ahead. 'What are you going to do?' she asked. 'Stop on here? I suppose you might become my brother's head gardener one day. If there continue to be such people, that is. But perhaps it would really come down to the turnips

– and to the two of you tugging them out and mashing them up together. That's my sister's vision of the future.'

'She might have a worse one.'

Much as if she had been a turnip herself, this pulled Patty up.

'It would be to chuck a lot on the scrap heap,' she said.

'Obviously. But I don't reckon there's any cause for alarm. Lady Lucy's fine, but just a bit doctrinaire. She's very young, of course.'

This was a moment of perfect agreement between these two mature persons. Boosie (at eighteen) was demonstrably very young. As for Swithin, he was rapidly becoming increasingly puzzling. But he was rapidly (although Patty didn't clearly formulate just how) becoming something else as well. It was with an entire lack of awkwardness that, in the interest of this sustained conversation, he had now desisted from his labours. He had been working hard, and there were tiny beads of perspiration on his forehead. He had an agreeable and slightly disturbing smell. His shirt-sleeves were rolled up to the armpit, and on the bronzed skin thus revealed glinted a fine powdering of golden hairs. These ought not to have suggested anything in particular to Lady Patience Wyndowe. But in fact they did. Had this encounter – she suddenly realized – ended only some moments ago she might have returned to the castle and blithely remarked to her mother that she had been flirting with Swithin Gore. It was something she would not now do.

'I might manage to get to a polytechnic,' Swithin said prosaically.

Patty's wild thought that she was perhaps falling in love with Swithin was far from rendered the less disconcerting by this announcement. Swithin as less garden boy than garden god was one thing; Swithin as hopeful postulant for some gruesome form of further education was quite another.

'Oh, Swithin,' Patty said, 'that would be perfectly splendid!' There was a small silence. It marked, on Swithin's part, a remorseless registering that she had, for the first time, said something stupid and insensitive; had, in fact, started villaging.

'It wouldn't exactly be high life,' Swithin said dryly. 'But it might he a foot in the door.'

'I meant something like that, Swithin. And I didn't mean to gush.'

Swithin, who had momentarily withdrawn tautly within himself, relaxed again. The effect, although not designed as extravagant, was rather that of a young Olympian in sudden effulgence. His glance, however, was less that of a divinity upon a mortal than of one operating the other way on. It was the wondering glance, more frankly accented this time than hitherto.

'That was very nice of you, Lady Patience,' he said.

'We must plan for it,' Patty said soberly. 'And my father would be interested, I know. Perhaps he isn't very informed about such things himself. But he's certain to know the people who are. Shall I – '

'Then I may speak to his lordship,' Swithin said calmly. 'If you think it a good idea, that is.' He paused. 'And now I'd better be getting on with the wallflowers. Perhaps you'll come and look at the effect later, m'lady.'

For a moment Patty felt that she had been abruptly dismissed. Then she realized that this wasn't the state of the case at all. She had known – clearly although through some bewilderment – that it was high time to bring this encounter to a close. And Swithin Gore, if he hadn't agreed, had understood. She hadn't been dismissed. She had been – for today she had been – let off.

4

Swithin Gore went on with his job of planting out the biennials. Whether he enjoyed doing so, or enjoyed his horticultural employment in general, we don't yet know. Nothing positively to throw light on the question have we heard pass between Lady Patience and himself. She, indeed, believes he takes pleasure in his work because if he didn't he wouldn't be as efficient at it as he is. This reasoning is insecure. The fact that Swithin hopes to go to a polytechnic tells us little. Everything under the sun is (in a fashion) taught in such places – including, perhaps, how to become a municipal gardener in a big way. Mr Pring, the head gardener at Mullion Castle and so Swithin's boss, would prefer his present situation to gardening all Bournemouth. But Mr Pring (like Dr Atlay, the vicar) has old-fashioned notions, and believes that there is something aristocratic about working for the aristocracy. There is no reason to suppose that Swithin Gore adopts this view – although he may, just at present, have a very decided motive for holding down his job with one particular aristocratic household.

Not that Swithin's job is under threat. Mr Pring thinks well of him, although he has at times been disposed to feel that the boy is a little too prone to keeping his own concerns and intentions firmly under his thatch. Indeed, Mr Pring thinks better of Swithin than he does of his other two assistants, since it is Swithin alone who can be relied upon to carry out instructions unmarred by ludicrous misconception. And even if Mr Pring disapproved of Swithin (as thinking too well of himself – which is the verdict upon him of his two fellows) it is probable that Swithin would get away with it. For of the Mullion household in its extended sense he is what an academic society would describe as a gremial member, having been born within the Mullion *protestas*, nurtured in its lap, bred up within its servitude, and thus assured of its protection. In fact there is an aspect of things, active at least in Lord Mullion's mind, in which Mr Pring himself, because hired in middle life, possesses a lesser status than Swithin Gore and other retainers to be judged of a hereditary order. This doesn't mean that Lord Mullion addresses more than a brief greeting to Swithin about half-a-dozen times in the twelvemonth. But he is aware of the lad, and would miss him if he cleared out – just as he would miss the disappearance from the castle of some inconsiderable piece of furniture that has been about for a long time.

Swithin, being clever, is aware of all this, but doesn't trade on it. He thinks that the Wyndowes, within the bounds set by the monstrous social injustices to which they subscribe, treat him decently enough, and probably did so from the start. He knows, without having to be told by Lady Patience, that if he makes a properly respectful approach to Lord Mullion access will be granted to him immediately and his ideas about a changed course of life will be entertained and sized up. But he knows he is still going to hesitate about this. He has somehow grown very fond of Mullion (although not of its wallflowers and other biennials in particular), and even if Lady Patience (Patty, he calls her to himself) were banished to Peru for keeps he would himself he reluctant to quit the place for good. He has a nebulous notion that he might even be trained to run it in the exalted station of its proprietor's agent – which, given the know-how, he believes he would be perfectly capable of doing. The snag about this daydream is Lord Wyndowe (whom he has no disposition to think of as Cyprian). Lord Wyndowe, as his father's heir, is only a heartbeat away from owning Mullion Castle and much else. And Swithin doesn't care for young Lord Wyndowe at all.

These thoughts, and certain others of a more elusive cast, were in Swithin's mind as he prepared to knock off for dinner. But there were more immediate and practical matters to think of as well. Heavy rainclouds were banking up in the west, and it looked as if the afternoon would see drenching summer rain. Pring had declared that it would infallibly hold off till nightfall. If this dogmatism proved unjustified Pring would be in a bad temper, and disposed in consequence to direct his subordinates to tasks as boring and disagreeable as he could think up. But there were various means of circumventing him here, in the deploying of which Swithin had developed considerable cunning. He was giving his mind to this as he walked down the drive in the direction of the main gates, some distance beyond which lay the cottage where he lodged. The route took him past the tennis court. Here he found something that arrested his attention.

On the previous afternoon there had been a tennis party going on. It had been his business to keep away from it, but he had heard a good deal of shouting and chatter and laughter, as well as the regular clop-clop of the balls, as he wheeled a gigantic amount of compost from one place to another. The net had now been let down and everything tidied up, except in one particular. On a garden chair lay a racket, with its press tossed down beside it. And also on the grass were a blazer, a sweater, and a long woollen scarf garishly striped. That was Cyprian Wyndowe, and the colours on display were no doubt a species of tribal emblem associated either with King's College, Cambridge, or with his lordship's earlier place of education. Lord Wyndowe didn't merely chuck things around all over the place; he expected them to be collected and fawningly brought back to him by whoever found them, much as if the entire staff of the castle were so many spaniels, retrievers, or similar canine serfs.

Swithin looked at these objects, and then looked up at the sky. There could now be no doubt about the rain; it might come pouring down at any moment. Swithin had no call to notice Lord Wyndowe's bits and pieces, but in the circumstances it seemed churlish and even bloody-minded to ignore them. He decided to collect them, proceed on his way, and return them to the castle when he went back to work. So he crossed the court (with which his own dealings were confined to cutting and rolling the turf and applying whitewash with meticulous care to its lines), screwed the racket into its press, and gathered the garments together and draped them around him. Then he went on his way.

He reached the main entrance to the castle grounds, and the lodge guarding it. The lodge, unlike the castle, had been built in an age in which symmetry was regarded as the only means to elegance, and it consisted of four diminutive rooms, each in a kind of pygmy Gothic, disposed two on one and two on the other side of the drive. This dwelling (or these dwellings) had no tenants, it having for long proved impossible to find human beings, however humble and however devoted to the Mullion name, to submit to a regular scamper through open air between supper and bed. Swithin had decided that when he took charge of things he would attach the one hutch to the other in the manner of Siamese twins – perhaps with a structure like the Rialto or (less ambitiously) the Bridge of Sighs as he had viewed these exotic structures in some picture-book.

Now he turned left, and passed on his left hand (since it lay not without but within the curtilage of the castle) Mullion parish church. The vicar, Dr Atlay, was standing in the porch, affixing to it a notice announcing sundry dates upon which no divine service would take place. Dr Atlay was aware of Swithin Gore as not among the devout, and was the more punctilious with a heartily unaffected greeting as a result. Swithin had no quarrel with heartily unaffected greetings, and responded by waving Lord Wyndowe's scarf. It would have been more appropriate, no doubt, to tug respectfully at a forelock – which was an object that a number of the older male inhabitants of Mullion continued to cultivate apparently to make this specific gesture of subjection possible. Swithin wound the scarf round his neck and walked on.

A wayfarer hove into view. He was approaching with a gait that suggested (if this be conceivable) resignation tempered by mild grievance, and he was not to be mistaken for other than gentry. He might have been about ages with Lord Mullion (whom Swithin thought of as distinctly elderly) and he was dressed in country clothes of the sort that indefinably suggest the townee. (Or so

Swithin, who cultivated social perceptions inappropriate to his station, sagely opined.)

The stranger drew near, hesitated, and came to a halt. He studied Swithin. At least Swithin felt it to be that, although the glance was in fact entirely momentary. It was – the young man somewhat confusedly felt – as if here was somebody with a trained eye of an unusual sort.

'Good morning,' the stranger said – and it was to be observed that his mild pedestrianism had put him slightly out of breath. 'Is it possible that I am speaking to Lord Wyndowe?'

'I'm not Lord Wyndowe. I'm one of the under-gardeners.' Swithin managed to provide this correction in a wholly composed manner, although he thought the question addressed to him excessively odd. Then he suddenly realized what must have occasioned it. Here he was, virtually within the purlieus of Mullion Castle, carrying a tennis racket and pretty well swathed in garments tagged all over with miscellaneous armorial emblazonments. He had, in fact, been sailing along under false colours. His first impulse was to explain to the stranger how this state of affairs had come about. But he resisted this – it is to be feared for no better reason than that it was more fun to leave the mystery momentarily unresolved. 'Can I help you in any way?' he asked. The stranger took this further perplexity (since the idiom was not quite a gardener's, whether under or otherwise) commendably in his stride.

'I don't want to be a nuisance,' he said. 'But the fact is that I've done something uncommonly stupid: run out of petrol the better part of a mile back. Can you tell me how far I am from Mullion Castle now?'

'Not all that far, sir. The gates are only a couple of hundred yards ahead of you. And then there's the drive through the park, which is just under half a mile.'

'Well, that's not too bad.' The stranger didn't seem to feel that it was too good either. 'I said I'd arrive in time for luncheon, and it seems uncivil to be late.'

'I could go ahead at the double, sir. It's really rather a nice run. I'd explain things. If you were to mention your name.'

'It's Charles Honeybath. I – '

'Mine's Swithin Gore.'

'How do you do?' Mr Honeybath said this instantly. 'But, no – I couldn't possibly trouble you in that way. If there were some petrol around, and I could be driven back with it to my car – '

'Is the key in the ignition?' It didn't seem to Swithin that the elderly Mr Honeybath was being too clear-headed.

'Yes, it is.'

'Then much better walk straight on to the castle, sir, and leave things to me. I think I can get hold of some petrol, and bring the car up to the castle not all that long after your own arrival. I do drive. I've driven his lordship's Rolls from time to time.' Swithin, who had his naive side, added this particular with some satisfaction. 'And you'd better start off at once, sir. I'm afraid it's going to rain rather heavily quite soon.'

'So it is.' Mr Honeybath glanced up at the heavens apprehensively. 'And it's uncommonly kind of you.' Mr Honeybath's hand moved towards a pocket, and then came away again. Swithin detected and approved this second thought. He didn't propose to be tipped by Mr Honeybath, either now or later. Payment for the petrol was one thing, and he'd make sure of collecting it. Accepting the price of a couple of drinks in return for giving an old buffer a helping hand was quite another. And now he hastened the old buffer on his way, and went about the business of retrieving his car. First Lord Wyndowe's tennis gear and now this visitor's stranded bus. He was doing the right thing about both of them, he told himself, like the model little lackey he was. He wondered, darkly, if Lord Mullion's elder daughter saw him that way.

5

An obliging young man, Charles Honeybath told himself as he walked on towards Mullion Castle. When explaining the manner of his arrival to his host and hostess he would not omit to express his sense of this strongly. For it must be said in general that disobligingness was abroad in the land, so that conduct of a contrary character deserved to be marked. It was true that the under-gardener called Swithin – an attractive name – had been amused as well as polite. But this was fair enough in face of that rash assumption that here had been Henry's son Cyprian. Moreover, stranded motorists are always for some reason mildly laughable, just as are equestrians who have tumbled off a horse. Honeybath imagined that upon socially appropriate occasions young Swithin might reveal a mildly satirical bent. It was possible that his mind was a little too lively for his job.

It suddenly became apparent that the lad was at least a good meteorologist. The rain was falling. In fact it might be said by a person of literary bent that the heavens had opened. And there was no shelter in sight. Along the hedgerow, indeed, there was a scattering of stately elms. But as these were all dead they were unlikely to afford much protection.

Honeybath hastened forward. The village of Mullion, he vaguely believed, lay some way ahead. But he must now be quite close to the entrance to the castle's drive, and there would probably be a lodge in which he could seek refuge for a time. If the rain were to prove continuous he could even remain there until Swithin turned up with his car. It looked as if Swithin's obliging disposition was going to earn him a good soaking at the start.

Honeybath became aware that there was, after all, a building in sight. It lay behind a high wall which had suddenly appeared on his right hand, so that its character was not immediately apparent. Honeybath was still in doubt about this when a head appeared above the wall and he found himself being addressed by a venerable clergyman.

'My dear sir,' the venerable clergyman said, 'can I not prevail upon you to enter the church?'

'Thank you. You are very kind.'

'Not at all. It is an invitation, alas, which I am well accustomed to addressing to those who ought to regard themselves as my parishioners. And now here I am – calling out, it may be said, in the highways and byways. Pray hasten, before you are soaked to the skin. There is an entrance, or better an aperture, only a few yards ahead. Strait is the gate, so far as our local people are concerned. The most imposing access to the churchyard is from the direction of the castle, naturally enough.'

Honeybath, not much regarding the element of chit-chat in this, hurried on and found the aperture. Within seconds he was inside the church itself. It was crepuscular and diminutive, the latter attribute being accented by the presence of a great deal of monumental and funerary sculpture of the more massive sort. He was incongruously reminded, indeed, of a doll's house lavishly equipped with furniture a size too large for it. But at least it was shelter, and Honeybath hastened to express his gratitude for this and to explain himself.

'A shocking downpour,' he then said. 'It was predicted by a young man who has now very kindly gone in search of petrol for me. I jumped to the rash conclusion that he must be Lord Mullion's son, but he proved to be one of the gardeners, and told me his name was Gore.'

'Ah, yes – Swithin Gore. I saw him myself only a little time ago, and he was good enough to wave to me.' The clergyman, who appeared to find this an amusing circumstance, glanced at Honeybath thoughtfully. 'You are on your way to the castle, sir?'

'I am on my way to stay there. But my immediate idea was to get as far as the drive and seek refuge in the lodge.'

'An idle thought, I fear. The lodge is empty and boarded up. The rich man is still in his castle, I am happy to say. But the poor man is no longer at his gate. *Tempora mutantur, et nos mutamur in illis.* May I mention that my name is Atlay? I am the incumbent.'

'How do you do? Honeybath is my name.'

'Ah, indeed!' Dr Atlay's features registered a kind of magisterial pleasure. 'I might have supposed it to be so, Mr Honeybath. Lord Mullion has mentioned to me that you were coming down. And upon what occasion. An excellent idea upon Mullion's part – as I told him at once. Nobody could do better justice to his wife than yourself, if I may venture a mere amateur's judgement upon such matters.'

'Thank you very much.' Honeybath didn't manage to say this particularly gratefully, since the receiving of formal compliments invariably irritated him. 'I don't know Lady Mullion very well, but she appears to be an admirable woman.'

'She is so, indeed – although not quite sound, I am sorry to say, upon the grand principle of subordination. It comes of belonging to a ducal house. Dukes are very odd fish, Mr Honeybath, as you have no doubt had abundant occasion to remark. Particularly when they are Whigs, as most of them are. Indeed, Mullion made a venturesome marriage, and I am inclined to regard as a matter of special dispensation by the Divine Providence the fact that it has been a happy one. There are two delightful daughters.'

'And a son, of course.'

'And, indeed, a son. I fear the rain is becoming, if anything, heavier.' Dr Atlay had paused to open the south door of the church and peer out. Hung on the door was a notice – addressed perhaps to the faithful or perhaps to casual gazers – saying *Please keep closed to conserve heat*, although in fact there was no visible provision for providing anything of the kind. 'However,' Dr Atlay continued, 'you and I are quite snug for the moment, Mr Honeybath. It is true that

31

the church is somewhat tenebrous and even speluncar in suggestion, a state of affairs attributable to the opaque quality achieved by Victorian stained glass – of which, I may say, we owe our abundance to the generosity of the eleventh earl. However, to his successor we owe similarly the repair of the roof, which is now watertight. So if light be excluded so, too, is the rage of the elements. You and I, my dear sir, may consider ourselves as cosily accommodated as Aeneas and Dido in their cavern.'

'Yes, indeed.' Honeybath was a little surprised by this pagan – and somewhat scandalous – comparison, which was no doubt to be attributed to the vicar's orthodox classical education. 'Are all those monuments and effigies,' he asked, 'connected with the Wyndowe family?'

'Assuredly they are – except, of course, that a number of my own predecessors are suitably commemorated on unobtrusive tablets in the chancel. The first Wyndowes, you will recall, were no more than knights of the shire, and the first whose sepulture is recorded here is Sir Rufus Windy. His is the figure on your right hand, with his nose broken off.'

Honeybath surveyed Sir Rufus with proper respect – but what he was then prompted to say was not untouched by levity.

'It has always struck me as odd, Dr Atlay, that in this matter of Christian burial it is the upper classes who enjoy God's chilly benediction, while their inferiors in this transitory state are out in the warm sun.'

'Ah!' If Dr Atlay was put momentarily to stand by this he recovered quickly. 'I do not recall that Shakespeare's application of the old saw is precisely to that effect. But you are, of course, perfectly right. The rude forefathers of the hamlet are out in the churchyard and certainly exposed to the elements – sun, wind and rain alike. However, that grand principle of subordination is involved. Are you familiar with the sermons of William Gilpin, as you doubtless are with his *Observations relative chiefly to picturesque beauty in the mountains and lakes of Cumberland and Westmoreland?*'

'I do know Gilpin on the Picturesque. He holds an important position – does he not? – in the history of English taste.' Honeybath felt that with Dr Atlay in learned vein it was necessary to put one's best foot forward. 'But his sermons, I am afraid, have escaped me.'

'They were published, I believe I am right in saying, in several volumes between 1799 and 1804. And in one of them he remarks that subordination pervades all the works of God. It is a profound truth not much regarded by modern theologians, I am sorry to conclude.'

Honeybath began to regret that he had accepted sanctuary as he had done. Had he walked on to the lodge, shut up though it might be, he could at least have cowered under its eaves until the arrival of Swithin in his car. As Swithin would now drive past the church unregarding, it looked to Honeybath as though he were booked to enjoy Dr Atlay's company until the tempest abated. Nor did he judge the topic upon which they had fallen particularly congenial. In an effort to find an alternative he now looked carefully round the gloomy little church. A number of its tombs and monuments, he felt, could be made to serve very tolerably as conversation pieces in the modern sense of the term. So he did his best to respond to such observations as were offered to him.

'As you will see,' Dr Atlay said, 'we are particularly rich in monumental work of the Elizabethan period. May I ask if it is a special interest of yours?'

'It is, indeed – but chiefly in the painting of the period, as you may imagine. And I am much looking forward to seeing the Mullion Hilliards. But dear me!' Honeybath had broken off, and was pointing to an ornate affair in the north aisle. 'Nollekens, surely? It can't be by anybody else.'

'Certainly Nollekens, and among the most distinguished of his works. Or so I have been told, although I must defer to your professional opinion, my dear sir. The reclining figure in classical drapery is, of course, a Countess of Mullion, and the medallion to which she points with upraised arm and extended index finger is naturally of her husband, the Earl. The weeping cherubs are much admired by our visitors. Remark how delicately their very tears are registered on the marble.'

Honeybath obediently studied Nollekens' blubbering brats. He had seen plenty of them before, and was rather fond of them. He read a long inscription enumerating the astounding virtues of the nobleman and his 'afflicted and disconsolate' wife. Then, guided by the vicar, he moved more or less systematically round the church. A Chinese gentleman, he reflected, unacquainted with the principles of the Christian religion or the purposes for which it built edifices like this one within which he found himself, would conjecture that here was a family mausoleum erected for the entombment of a line of persons who had richly merited a far more resplendent resting-place – and this less because of their inherited rank than of their unfailing eminence as models and exemplars to society as a whole. The Tudors in quaint verses, the Augustans in balanced and cadenced prose, and between these the Elizabethan lords of language and their intricately conceited Jacobean successors: all these celebrated, in words incised in marble, sundry Wyndowes as very paragons, marks, and cynosures of their time. Even the present earl's grandfather, who had lived on into the year 1906, was described as having been solicitous for the welfare of the deserving poor; and his successor, Sylvanus Wyndowe, Lord Mullion, was commemorated not only as a Lord Lieutenant and a Knight of the Garter but also as a conscientious Chairman of the Mullion and Little Lintel Rural District Council. And then, after all this Rococo twiddliness and verbal orotundity, Honeybath noticed a small plaque which read simply: RUPERT WYNDOWE LORD WYNDOWE, followed by two dates from which it was to be inferred that Rupert Wyndowe Lord Wyndowe had survived only into his thirty-sixth year. He was that uncle of Henry's, Honeybath recalled, who would have succeeded to the earldom had he not predeceased his father.

'Rupert's memorial,' he said to Dr Atlay, 'is surely on the reticent side?'

'Indeed, yes. He might have been a mere vicar of the parish.'

'Dear me! Did he, in fact, take holy orders?'

'No. It was decidedly not a course of life that would have entered Rupert Wyndowe's head. And that, perhaps, was just as well. It may have been injudicious of the late earl to commemorate his elder brother so ostentatiously sparely – if the expression is a permissible one. But Rupert's short life had been far from uniformly edifying, I am sorry to say. The family would not, at the time, have regarded it as at all suitable for – as one might express it – window-dressing.' Dr Atlay frowned, as if conscious that the lure of this somewhat laboured witticism (which had nothing classical about it) had led him into a minor impropriety. Rupert Wyndowe, after all, had been a close relative of the present earl, and ought not to be exhibited as a bad hat to a stranger only just encountered. It was true that Lord Mullion had not yet been born at the time of his uncle's untimely decease; and, further, that this distinguished portrait painter had apparently some claim to be Lord Mullion's intimate friend. But a gossiping approach to family history had been indelicate, all the same.

Charles Honeybath, unfortunately, seemed to be unaware of this regard for the higher seemliness of things. He continued to look thoughtfully at Rupert Wyndowe's commemorative tablet.

'Perhaps,' he said, 'it may be considered only as an interim measure or holding operation? Black sheep are often brought back into family esteem after no more than a couple of generations – their shabby tricks taking on a patina of endearing foible. Unspeakable reprobates are in a different category, so that a couple of centuries may pass before their descendants start taking pride in them. And I imagine this Rupert Wyndowe to have been of the former sort.'

'Oh, entirely so.' The vicar was clearly not going to be tempted into further disclosures about the obscurely unsatisfactory uncle of the present Earl of Mullion. 'I take it, Mr Honeybath, that most of the family as now constituted is known to you fairly well?'

'Far from it. Mullion and I have been in the habit of meeting from time to time – but more on the strength of past associations, which were extremely agreeable, than of common interests now. And of course I have made the acquaintance of his wife. But the rest of the people down here are strangers to me.'

'You will at least find them not so numerous as to be confusing. It is to be regretted that there are no younger sons. There ought always, to my mind, to be younger sons in any family of consequence.'

'No doubt. But I imagine that the more one feels oneself to be of consequence the more of a problem may younger sons present. You can't set them to the plough-tail, even if that would be their natural mark.' Even as he uttered this small acerbity Honeybath was a little ashamed of it. His wife had died childless long ago, and he had done nothing to provide himself with children since. Yet he would have liked to have a son, and had this been granted to him he would at least have brought up the boy not to suppose himself the owner of any consequence he hadn't earned. But he mustn't, he told himself, be irked by Dr Atlay, who had been his Good Samaritan in a sense, and whose devotion to what used to be called the landed interest had at least no vice to it. Honeybath, moreover, made most of his living out of people of consequence. So it wasn't for him to quarrel with the traditional set-up of English society – or even, if it came to a pinch, with what Atlay described as the grand principle of subordination. 'I gather,' he said, 'that Mullion is troubled only by one younger brother, the Sylvanus of the present generation.' In talking to this cleric, who doubtless regarded himself as primarily a kind of domestic chaplain to the Wyndowes, Honeybath seemed to have settled for 'Mullion' – which was less formal than 'Lord Mullion' but less intimate than 'Henry'. Nothing, he thought, is more tricky in an entirely trivial way than this particular area of nomenclature. For example, he was presumably going to be introduced to a lady whom Henry would casually name 'my Great-aunt Camilla'. But was she 'Lady Camilla Wyndowe', or 'the Hon. Camilla Wyndowe' (which one would have to know if one was going to address a letter to her), or just plain 'Miss'? It was a question not answerable until one had worked it out that she was the daughter of a younger son of an earl, and even then some complicating factor might have provided her with a handle to her name. Honeybath was about to make an inquiry about Camilla when he recalled Lord Mullion as having said something to the effect that this aged kinswoman was off her head. So he stuck to Sylvanus instead. 'I've gathered,' he said, 'that Mullion's brother lives in the dower house. Is he a married man?'

'Yes, indeed – and with three daughters. Sylvanus Wyndowe came out of the army several years ago, and is now our local MFH. A very jolly fellow. One can scarcely glance at him without thinking of beef and ale.'

'Dear me!'

' "Ruddy" would he the first word to occur to me were I endeavouring to describe the outward man. And he goes in for roaring.'

'Roaring?'

'Just that. A squirearchal type of the old school. One would scarcely associate him with the higher nobility. There is perhaps a touch of affectation about it. But he is a most agreeable fellow, and you will enjoy his company.'

Honeybath wished he could feel assured of this. He judged that he might prove rather allergic to being roared at. But as the thought crossed his mind something not totally dissimilar happened to him in the form of a loud summons from what he recognized as the horn of his own motor car.

'Bless my soul!' he exclaimed. 'It must be that young man.' And without much ceremony he hurried to the church door and pulled it open. The rain was still falling – but there, only a dozen yards away, was Swithin Gore with his car. Swithin, perhaps exhilarated by his position at its wheel, seemed unconscious that there had been anything peremptory about his behaviour.

'Here you are, sir!' he now shouted. 'I guessed you might have dodged in there. So come along, and you may still be in time for the soup.'

Honeybath, who was far from taking umbrage at this brisk behaviour, signalled his acquiescence, renewed his expressions of gratitude to Dr Atlay, and then ran for the car. It was a new car, and in acquiring it he had for some reason treated himself to a vehicle of a distinctly superior order. It obviously pleased Swithin very much, so Honeybath insisted that Swithin should continue to drive.

Swithin drove far from rashly, and they were through the castle gates and inside the park before he relaxed sufficiently to speak.

'Didn't you know,' he asked wonderingly, 'that there's a reserve tank?'

'A reserve tank?'

'Didn't you see that little red light? It's off again now, but it must have been on for quite a long time. It tells you the main tank is emptying.'

'It was most unobservant of me, I fear.' Honeybath might have been disconcerted, or even offended, by this ruthless exposure of his incompetence. But Swithin's pleasure, imperfectly dissimulated, in his own superior knowledge was infectious rather than irritating.

'What you have to do is flick down that switch.' Swithin took a hand briefly from the wheel the more certainly to elucidate this mystery.

'Then the red light goes off, and the green one above it comes on as it is now. It's to continue to remind you that you're now on the reserve tank. And that's a gallon and a half.'

'I see. Thank you very much.'

'You won't forget?' Swithin asked seriously.

'No, I promise not to forget.'

'No use having those superior gadgets, sir, if you don't master them.'

'Perfectly true.'

It was thus that a chastened Charles Honeybath arrived, chauffeur-driven, at Mullion Castle.

6

Swithin's hope was fulfilled, and Honeybath was in time for the soup. He suspected, indeed, that it had been put back for half an hour in the continued expectation of his arrival. And it was pretty well all that *had* been put back, since the Mullions' luncheon, although attended by several servants, consisted of an unassuming *potage du jour* followed by bread and cheese.

'I'm sure you won't mind falling in with our ways, Charles,' Lord Mullion said by way of commenting on this. 'On wholly domestic occasions, that's to say. The fact is that when one's getting on what one comes to appreciate is a single slap-up meal in the day.'

'I quite agree,' Honeybath said. 'As the perspectives shorten, one doesn't want to spend one's afternoons half-asleep.'

'No, indeed,' Lady Mullion said briskly. And her glance upon her guest and prospective portraitist was, for the first time, definitely approving.

'So we dine,' Lord Mullion pursued with a hint of apology, 'in what you might call an almost formal way. Black tie, Charles, if it isn't too much of a bore.'

'Not at all. Every wise man still carries such a thing around.'

'A damned funny thing.' Cyprian Wyndowe interjected at this point. 'A chap at King's – an up-and-coming prole – got an invitation from the Provost's wife or somebody saying "Black tie". He hadn't a notion it meant a dinner-jacket – '

'And why should he?' Boosie Wyndowe interrupted. 'It's a perfectly idiotic expression.'

'And he probably didn't own such a thing, anyway. So he turned up in an imitation London suit, and an enormous sailor's knot black tie, as if the wretched woman's dinner party was a funeral.'

'And now we all laugh,' Boosie said. 'O God, O Montreal!'

Lord and Lady Mullion, unfamiliar with the poetry of the second Samuel Butler, looked perplexed. They must have been conscious, too, Honeybath supposed, of a certain callow quality in their son and heir's notion of an entertaining anecdote. But Lord Mullion pursued his theme unruffled.

'After all,' he said, 'one must wash. And if one washes one might as well change. So I've no quarrel with a black tie. And Camilla usually comes down to dine with us, you know, and she likes it. Or I'm not sure that she does. *White* ties every night would be her thing. At least we've got away from all that, except at those big vulgar does. Great-aunt Camilla is Victorian to the core.'

'With the justification, I imagine, of having been born in that reign?' Honeybath said.

'I rather think not quite. Mary, would that be right?'

'It's almost impossible to say – at least if one believes what *she* says.' Lady Mullion spoke on a note of affectionate amusement. 'She claims to have been born on the day the Old Queen died. But it's not a point I've checked up on – as I've had to do so often with so many of you Wyndowes.'

'Perhaps the ancient creature fancies herself as a prompt reincarnation of that tough old Teuton,' Cyprian said, and paused as if to have this sally admired. Nothing of the sort happening he added. 'I'd have supposed her a good deal older, as a matter of fact.'

'Splendidly ageless, really,' Lady Patience Wyndowe said. 'But I do think of her as belonging to a time quite out of mind.'

'As at your age, my dear Patty, you may well do.' Lord Mullion paused while digging a spoon vigorously into a Stilton. 'But nothing of the kind. I believe our worthy vicar, for example, could give her ten years or thereabout. Did Martin Atlay entertain you to any family history, Charles?'

'Very moderately. We did a short round of the Wyndowe monuments.'

'He'd know all about them. And he knows all about us. If puzzled, Charles, ask Atlay. He's a historically minded chap.'

'I might have heard more if the young man hadn't turned up so smartly with my car.' Honeybath recalled his resolution to be emphatically commendatory about the young man. 'He was quite uncommonly efficient and friendly.'

'Glad to hear it, Charles. Was it Gore, did you say? A promising lad, I believe, and certainly not morose like so many of them. Willing, if not particularly bright, I imagine.'

'Swithin Gore is very bright indeed, papa.' Patty had come out with this swiftly – and struck Honeybath as instantly surprised, and perhaps annoyed, that she had done so.

'Agreed,' Boosie said. 'I've flirted with Swithin like mad, and his heart is quite gorgeously adamant. He's amused, but he knows everything not to do or say. Which doesn't hold of all Eton and King's – or not in *my* experience.'

This extravagance didn't please young Lord Wyndowe, who said something crude about pig-tailed brats looking for kicks from clod-hoppers. Honeybath suspected it didn't please Patty either. It certainly didn't please her mother, who changed the subject.

'I'm so glad, Mr Honeybath, that you have turned up today and not tomorrow. Wednesdays are terribly restless, and Saturdays are, too.'

'Ah, yes, Charles!' Lord Mullion broke in. 'I was going to tell you, wasn't I? The place is open to the public on those days, and at this time of year they pile in like mad. It's quite a problem. We can't hide in the attics, because that's where Prince Rupert lodged his officers and held his councils of war. There are maps on the walls and cannon-balls in the fireplaces and even plumed hats on the clothes pegs. So they all have to be shown, and we have to skulk where we can.'

'Or be shown ourselves,' Boosie said.

'Just so, my dear. I sometimes wish we'd remained papists for longer than we did, and had provided the castle with a clutch of priest's holes. They'd come in handy.' This was evidently one of Lord Mullion's well-worn jokes. 'However, I think we can hide you away, Charles.'

'Perhaps,' Cyprian said, 'Mr Honeybath would like to pay at the turnstile and be taken round.'

For the first time since his arrival, Honeybath observed Lord Mullion to frown. Rightly or wrongly, he had regarded this sally of his son's as hinting insolence.

'Don't be foolish, Cyprian. And, by the way, please don't do just that again yourself. Once or twice was a passable joke, but after that it involves a lack of consideration to the people who are good enough to help us run the thing.'

'Very well, sir.' Cyprian, although not pleased at being publicly rebuked, looked at his father without resentment. Honeybath told himself that here was a household getting along with no more than moderate friction. If anyone went in for belligerency it was probably Boosie. And, indeed, Boosie had a fling now.

'Cyprian,' she explained to Honeybath, 'paid at the door, and attached himself to a party, and kept on asking silly questions. It was an old friend of the family, Miss Kinder-Scout, who was taking round that particular lot, and of course she knew Cyprian perfectly well. She must have been rather upset.'

'It must certainly have been a little surprising.'

'But he did something sillier still.' Lady Lucy Wyndowe (to give Boosie her proper name) seemed not a particularly tactful child, and she had a sisterly indictment to press home. 'He'd taken care to leave his own silver cigarette case on a table in the library, and when he thought that Miss Kinder-Scout wasn't looking and that several visitors were, he put out a stealthy hand and pocketed the thing. One flinches from the thought of peering inside the head of anybody who could put on so idiotic a turn.'

'It was an experiment in the psychology of crowd behaviour,' Cyprian said calmly. 'You know what one reads about it. Half a dozen people see a silver-haired old gentleman being robbed, or a blind beggar being beaten up, or a girl being raped – '

'Cyprian, dear,' Lady Mullion said.

'Well, anything of that sort. And half a dozen people look on and do nothing about it, because some completely inhibitory mechanism takes charge. And that's what happened here.'

'But not for long, as you perfectly well know,' Boosie said. 'For Miss Kinder-Scout had seen you after all, and she'd had enough. So she called out in that rather loud voice she has: "Lord Wyndowe, I am glad to see you have found the cigarette case you mislaid." And I suppose the party took you for a harmless family lunatic.'

'We're pretty well furnished in that line already, aren't we?' Cyprian asked. Then he turned to his father. 'By the way, sir, what are we going to do about providing Mr Honeybath with a studio?'

'Excellent question.' Lord Mullion was plainly relieved that the late slightly unbecoming exchanges were over. 'Only we mustn't hurry Honeybath into a decision about anything of that kind. Charles, I'm sure you'll want to get to know the place a bit for a start?'

'Decidedly, Henry. And, Lady Mullion, you – '

'Mary – please.'

'And you, Mary, may have your own orders to give. I seem to remember Henry speaking of your portrait as being required for hanging on the other side of the fireplace from his. But I suspect he was being funny.'

'Oh, definitely,' Lord Mullion said. 'Or call it *une façon de parler*, Charles. I just felt we ought both to be done, you know.'

'Quite so. And if the one portrait needn't control the other, then Mary can choose between various possibilities. A neutral background, for example, or a formal and traditional one – '

'Marble pillars,' Boosie said. 'improbably draped with velvet curtains and gold tassels? She won't want that.'

'Or a favourite corner of a room, or the open air,' Honeybath concluded.

'Under the castle chestnut tree the castle beauty stands,' Patty said. 'I vote for that. Or I would if we had a chestnut tree – which I don't think we do. But what about a dress, Mr Honeybath? May my mother choose that?'

'Ah, there we come on delicate ground.' Honeybath was well-acquainted with this sort of chatter, and believed himself to have a modest skill in treating it lightly. 'But one can come to an accommodation with women in a way one often can't with men. Men have all those absurd and inflexible fancy-dresses that Virginia Woolf made fun of. Uniforms and mayoral gowns and doctoral robes. It would be all right if they didn't have complexions – often confoundedly pronounced complexions – as well. Monkey with the hue of the uniform and they treat you as if you were a fraudulent military tailor. Tackle the problem through the complexion and they accuse you of representing them either as dipsomaniac or at death's door. Be compliant and the critics laugh at you – and fairly enough. Painters are like policemen. Their lot is not a happy one.'

This little routine on the mysteries of art was well received, and stimulated the younger Wyndowes to various jocose suggestions. Cyprian expressed the hope that Honeybath wouldn't insist on his mother being paraded in all the Mullion diamonds, since this would result in the embarrassing disclosure that his father had been constrained to put them quietly up the spout. Boosie, who didn't approve of this flight of fancy, advanced one of her own – to the effect that her mother might be represented signing a cheque to pay off her brother's embarrassments of a different character at Cambridge and elsewhere. Lady Mullion, seeing the conversation thus veer again towards family pleasantry of an undesirable sort, rose and said firmly that they would take coffee on the terrace.

Castles are not properly provided with terraces, or not of a formally balustraded kind. But Mullion had been adorned with this amenity by filling in part of the moat on the south side. Lord Mullion went into a routine of his own about this. The moat, he explained, was quite bogus, after all. It had been dug out at the time the Wyndowes had been allowed to crenellate, and licence for that had come only when castles were pretty well finished, anyway. Even Prince Rupert hadn't been fool enough to think to hold Mullion; he had persuaded the sixth earl to cede it gracefully, and had followed this up by himself briskly winning several minor skirmishes in its neighbourhood. Boosie said that this hadn't amounted to much, and that extensive reading had brought her to the conclusion that the Cavaliers had been a pretty button-headed lot. Wily peers had gone with the other crowd, like the people over at Broughton Castle in the next county. Patty said that a family ought to stick by its own order, and a lively debate – this time blessedly impersonal – followed. Honeybath began to wonder whether the repose essential for the labours of artistic creation was going to be readily obtainable at Mullion Castle. But he was a man rather short of acquaintance among the spirited young, and was disposed to be well contented with his entertainment so far.

7

In the early afternoon Lady Mullion took Honeybath round the castle. It was a little tour made with a minimum of historical expatiation, and would probably have been regarded as inadequate by any of the hard-working ladies who performed the job on a professional basis on Wednesdays and Saturdays. But then one's friends, as distinct from one's customers, are not to be regarded as avid for their pennyworth of information. Faintly in Lady Mullion's attitude, too, there could be detected a feeling that there wasn't, after all, a great deal to show off. Mullion Castle was an interesting old place, and she had with a proper marital loyalty become extremely fond of it. But a medieval castle, even when it had been given an Elizabethan face-lift on one façade and some further Jacobean flourishes here and there, remained a slightly quaint place to live in. Honeybath felt a mild puzzle here until he recalled Lady Mullion's own background. The Wyndowes weren't all that in the way of ancientry, the original Sir Rufus Windy himself being very much a post-Conquest man. Even so, they were a whole lot older-established than Lady Mullion's own family, which had bobbed up only under Queen Anne. Then, however, it had bobbed up fast and far, and for many generations now had dwelt amid a Palladian magnificence unexcelled in England. So deep in Lady Mullion's mind was the thought that Mullion Castle was a kind of *cottage orné* in which it was rather fun to perch in a consciously modest way.

It was, however, clear to Honeybath that the small expedition, from which the rest of the household had absented itself, had been contrived for the purpose of introducing him less to his surroundings than to a closer acquaintance with Lady Mullion herself. His mission, or commission, being as it was, this was entirely sensible, and witnessed on the lady's part to a sound instinct as to what portrait-painting was about. It wasn't that she felt herself in any aggressive way as having a personality to exhibit. She knew perfectly well, indeed, that Honeybath's own personality was as important a constituent of the proposed exercise as her own. There was a rapport to establish, and this was as pleasant a way of establishing it as any offering.

'There must have been a certain liveliness here at that time,' Lady Mullion said when they were examining some of the memorials of the brief tenancy of the castle by Prince Rupert, Count Palatine of the Rhine. 'I never much care for being away from Mullion, but we do have a quiet time. I have to be glad that I'm not one who hungers after what they call scope.'

'I suspect that you keep yourself fairly busy, Mary.'

'Well, yes – in a sense. People sometimes think of this sort of life as all luxurious idleness. I glimpse it occasionally in the expressions of our dollar-a-time visitors. But there is hard work, in a way, in just keeping the thing going. And Henry would do anything to manage that. Perhaps it's something that the women of our sort feel less than the men – I suppose because the women have to pack their bags and hump it to a new home on marriage. Do you know, Charles? I have a recurrent dream in which the castle goes up in flames. That's very shocking in me, of course. But we all rush around with buckets and hoses, and it's tremendous fun. At least a happening, as they say.'

'I doubt whether you'd actually much enjoy anything of the kind.' Honeybath had been a little startled by this harmless confidence. 'But I do see the merit of a happening now and then.'

'I believe I could make do with a ghost. Our vicar, Dr Atlay, whom you've met, says there is a ghost. Only it doesn't seem to care for the twentieth century, and hasn't been showing up. Once or twice I've imagined I was encountering it: a tall gliding figure in white. But it has turned out to be Great-aunt Camilla in one of her wandering moods.'

'I hope you didn't reveal your disappointment to her.' Honeybath produced this slightly facetious response as preferable to silence and likely to keep the topic of the reclusive Miss Wyndowe alive. He felt, indeed, that Lady Mullion had introduced the ghost into her conversation by way of thus going on to speak of this aged relative. He was to be given his bearings on her.

'It certainly mightn't be too cheering to be told one had been mistaken for a ghost. But Camilla is little unaccountable at the best of times, and might be gratified. She might even be prompted to the conclusion that she was a ghost. I am sure she will interest you, Charles. But should she say anything to offend you, you will remember that she is slightly strange.'

'So I've gathered. Henry told me that at one time Miss Wyndowe was devoted to painting.'

'Yes, indeed – although she gave it up long ago. As a young woman, I believe, she had serious thoughts of making a profession of it. She went to Paris to study – which was quite a dashing thing to do at that time – and then spent several months in Provence as the pupil of some artist she particularly admired. He advised her to continue her travels and make a thorough job of Italy. That may have been because he saw real promise in her, or because she was being a nuisance and he wanted to be rid of her. Neither explanation would surprise me.'

'And she did go to Italy?'

'Apparently not. She turned the idea down out of hand, on religious grounds.'

'How very odd!'

'Great-aunt Camilla was in those days a most convinced Protestant. She could put up with Catholicism in France, she said, because it is independent there and not really papistical. But she wouldn't enter territory which she believed to be wholly dominated by somebody she termed the so-called Bishop of Rome.'

'Miss Wyndowe sounds like one who knows her own mind. But it seems sad that she should have deprived herself of the Uffizi and the Sistine Chapel on such rigidly doctrinal lines.'

'She might have tolerated the Uffizi if a magic carpet could have transported her there. But she would certainly have pictured the Sistine Chapel as thronged with cardinals and with the Pope sitting in the middle of them.'

'Dear me!' Honeybath was amused by this conception. 'I wonder what she would have thought of the Archbishop of Canterbury having a little *tête-à-tête* with His Holiness bang in front of that Last Judgement.'

'You must ask her.'

'Would it not be injudicious to advance upon religious topics when conversing with her?'

'My dear Charles, it is impossible to be either judicious or injudicious with Camilla Wyndowe. Because you never know what will take her how.' Lady Mullion paused upon this brisk locution. 'She's mysterious,' she suddenly added.

'You fill me with curiosity. But mysterious in what sense?'

'I haven't expressed myself too well. There's no mystery-mongering to her. It's simply that I've always felt that some mystery attaches to her. She has a secret. Or she *is* somebody's secret. Something like that.'

'I'd like to see some of this remarkable lady's paintings.'

'She might be persuaded to produce a portfolio of them. We have two or three of them framed and hung up, for that matter. I imagine they don't quite rank with the Hilliards. They may be in one of the service corridors, along with people's favourite horses and dogs, and things of that kind. You will find, by the way, that the castle is simply jam-packed with junk. When Cyprian makes that silly joke about the pawned family diamonds he often adds that our fortunes will be retrieved by the discovery of some enormously valuable Chinese vases in a potting shed. Hasten the day – although I don't really believe it.' Lady Mullion glanced at her watch. 'It's time for tea, Charles. If tea doesn't – as it does Henry – bore you.'

'By no means. I look forward to it all day, and now it will recruit me for a little stroll outside afterwards. The rain seems over and gone.' Honeybath was not unused to being a solitary guest in country houses, and knew the various approved ways of making oneself scarce at appropriate times. One announced the need to attend to one's correspondence, or an urge to take a turn in the park or explore the village.

'They ring a bell at half past seven,' Lady Mullion said comprehendingly. 'To give time for that black tie. And at eight o'clock Camilla, if she feels like it, comes down in her lift. A kind of *dea ex machina*.'

'To reveal the truth of things and generally clear matters up?'

'Possibly, I suppose. But it hasn't happened yet.'

8

Honeybath's stroll through the park by which Mullion Castle was now surrounded prolonged itself beyond his first intention, but he felt that his time was his own until the moment came to think of that black tie. After the rain it was a flawless late afternoon to which the earlier downpour had lent the enchantment of a sparkle of moisture scattered like Constable's snow over the scene. Francis Kilvert, he felt, that superb landscape painter *manqué*, might have done justice to it in his incomparable diary. Many of Kilvert's favourite effects were on view: in the distance bluish hills; nearer at hand the shadows of great trees elongating themselves on the grass; numerous contented kine; here and there less numerous rustics making their unassuming way home after the labours of the day; the glint and murmur of a half-hidden stream. Presently would come still Evening on, and Twilight gray would in her sober livery all things clothe. All in all, it was a peaceful scene, admirably adapted to mild literary musings of this sort.

Honeybath paused to admire a noble barn. It stood on a spot, some hundred yards ahead, on the verge of arable land into which the park here merged without any notable boundary. It was an antique barn, speaking perhaps of monastic opulence long ago. Now, no doubt, it was Lord Mullion's property. Honeybath advanced again, resolved to take a closer view of this venerable pile in its spacious and tranquil setting. Then, abruptly, he came once more to a halt, for the general decorum of the scene had been suddenly and most hideously disturbed. Moments before, the air had held nothing but a solemn stillness tempered by the soft susurration of the wind in the trees. Now from the interior of the barn there was issuing a howling and wailing as of some living creature in atrocious pain. And it was accompanied by a sound, metronomic in its regularity, which powerfully rekindled in Honeybath his worst memories of Draconian prefectorial attentions during his earlier years at school. In short, within the barn somebody was receiving an uncommonly vigorous walloping.

Charles Honeybath was not the man hastily to intrude upon any episode of unseemly violence. If an irate farmer were chastising some urchin caught stealing turnips the incident, although distressing and contrary to the liberal and humanitarian spirit of the age, was no business of his. But it was clearly not an urchin that was involved. The dire screeching and yelling – perhaps, as often in such cases, pitched a little in excess of actual need – was issuing, he felt sure, from a female throat. Chivalrously aroused, Honeybath hastened into the barn. A shocking spectacle met his eyes. On a bale of hay there was sitting a powerful male character belonging obviously to the lower reaches of rustic society. Across his knees he held down a young female who was not precisely a child. And he was at choice intervals belabouring her person, appropriately exposed, not indeed with any instrument of correction whether improvised or other, but with a bare hand as large and heavy as a ham.

'You scoundrel, stop that instantly!' Honeybath, although profoundly shocked, found himself adequately articulate at once. 'Desist!' he added, as if to make his meaning more abundantly clear.

The rural executioner, thus adjured, raised his arm again in air – and there maintained it immobile for a moment, as if himself poised between astonishment and augmented rage. Whereupon his victim, profiting smartly from this brief indecision, wriggled free and made a dash past Honeybath for liberty, pulling a scanty skirt down to her knees as she ran. Although but briefly glimpsed, she was revealed to Honeybath as an ungainly trollop in her latest teens, or possibly even a little older than that. This circumstance, although it perhaps enhanced the high impropriety of what had been going on, in fact a little relieved Honeybath's mind. Even as the man jumped to his feet and pursued the escaping young woman with a shout of rage, he arrived at the swift perception that this was a family affair. It was a father who had thus been so vigorously correcting his child. Perhaps he even had some legal entitlement to such drastic behaviour: it must depend on his daughter's actual age. Both of them were now half-way across the nearest field, and the man was waving his arms less with a suggestion of further castigation than of a labourer herding an escaped heifer in some desired direction. Parent and child were in fact on their way home.

Honeybath, who had at least a reading man's knowledge of the *mores* of rural society, felt little doubt as to the prompting occasion of what he had interrupted. So clear was he about this that he looked about him for a second and probably younger man. Even as he did so he heard a sound behind him, turned round, and found himself confronting Swithin Gore. Where Swithin had bobbed up from he didn't know, but it seemed a rational inference that it was from some hastily achieved hiding place under the hay at the other end of the barn. What Honeybath had stumbled upon – or what the outraged parent had stumbled upon perhaps only minutes before – was an episode of youthful incontinence somewhat in the spirit of *Tom Jones*.

'Just what have you been up to?' Honeybath demanded. Being extremely displeased, he spoke with a sternness wholly unwarranted by his standing in the affair. He had, after all, no title whatever to set himself up as a censor of this youth's morals, however deplorable they might have revealed themselves to be. But earlier that day he had taken a liking to his highly competent rescuer, and now he was oddly disappointed in the estimate he had formed of him.

'Up to?' Swithin repeated coldly. 'I was walking past. I don't say I didn't know what was going on, or liked what followed. But I have to keep my place.'

'I don't believe you.' Honeybath must have been very upset to make this rash remark. And Swithin was very upset too; in fact he was angry, confused, and humiliated. And now he said nothing more. He gave Honeybath a single brief icy look which the painter was to remember. And then he walked away.

In this uncomfortable moment Honeybath again became aware that he was not alone. With much the same effect that Swithin had given of appearing from nowhere, a middle-aged man was now standing just inside the barn door. His complexion was sanguine – so brilliantly so, indeed, that Honeybath's first confused impression had been of some threatening incendiary disaster within the building. For a brief instant the newcomer appeared disconcerted and uncertain of his ground. Then, hard upon this, he rapidly disposed his features on lines of the most theatrically emphatic ferocity.

'Who the devil are you?' he bellowed.

Not unnaturally, Honeybath was disconcerted in his turn – and not the less so from an immediate conviction that here was another Wyndowe. The resemblance, indeed, to the members of the family already known to him was subtle, almost fugitive, rather than pronounced. But here was territory to which Honeybath carried a professional eye, and he had no doubt about the matter whatever. At the same time he was fleetingly aware of an elusive element of *déjà vu* in the perception, and this he might have identified had not another idea instantly occurred to him. The violent character had bellowed. In fact, he had *roared*. He must be Henry's younger brother, Sylvanus Wyndowe.

'Too much damned trespassing around these days,' Mr Wyndowe continued in a voice still pitched as if to carry across a parade ground. 'Snooping, as well. A confounded little Paul Pry. No bloody business of yours, what local people may be up to.'

Honeybath might have said something chilling like 'I happen, sir, to be Lord Mullion's guest.' But for the moment he said nothing at all, being entirely occupied in essaying some interpretation of Sylvanus Wyndowe's behaviour and comportment. Sylvanus might have been said to be blustering – except that he couldn't be felt as subject to the sort of failure in self-confidence which is the common prompting to anything of the kind. While offering his string of disobliging remarks he had been engaged, with gestures perfectly composed, in brushing down his well-worn tweeds and removing straws from his hair. Yes, actually that! And what he was flicking from those Savile Row garments was nothing more nor less than hay seeds! Upon this there could be only one rational conclusion. It was Sylvanus Wyndowe, and not his brother's gardener's boy, who had been constrained to dive into ignominious hiding when interrupted by that outraged parent in the prosecution of a low amour. Honeybath knew that he ought to be very shocked by this discovery. But it was a state of affairs so ludicrous that he quite failed for the moment to conjure up this correct response. He was chiefly conscious of dismay that he had done Swithin Gore wrong.

'Sir,' he managed to say with dignity, 'it may well be that I have intruded. But I am happy to say that my intervention at least cut short the most barbarous behaviour to a young woman on the part of one of those "local people" you have referred to.'

'Belting the little bitch, wasn't he?' With disconcerting abruptness, Sylvanus had switched from fury to merriment. The effect was of a wild hilarity caught up and magnified by some public address system. 'Good heavens, man, you can't stop that sort of thing! It's immemorial in a peasantry. You can have a fellow up before a whole bench of beaks who are your own best neighbours, and complain that he has been larruping his brats like hell within the hearing of your maiden aunt. They'll do no more than admonish the brute – and for your pains you'll find yourself ill-regarded in half a dozen villages around you. Did you ever read Kilvert's *Diary*?'

'More than once, most certainly.' Honeybath was startled by this telepathic cropping up of a work that had been in his own head not half an hour before.

'Milk-and-water sort of parson, although damned agreeable in his own way. But he quite takes for granted his parishioners lamming into their brats like mad. Even offers to lend a hand once, if I remember aright.'

'There was a slight strain of morbidity in Kilvert, no doubt.' Honeybath, although much displeased by this brazen talk on the part of a profligate wretch such as he judged Sylvanus Wyndowe to be, had to acknowledge that he was a man of education. 'But common decency,' he added grimly, 'requires that we shouldn't ourselves precipitate such behaviour.'

'I don't know what you're talking about.' It was quite clear that Sylvanus in fact did. Indeed, it was possible to suspect that he might have been detected as blushing, had his customary hue not been such as to render anything of the sort indetectable. 'And confound your impudence,' Sylvanus added, with a return to his earlier manner.

'Confound your own, sir!' It was with a not unreasonable warmth that Honeybath delivered this just retort. But he recalled that here was his host's brother, whom it was very possible that he would later be constrained to meet within a family circle. It seemed judicious, therefore, to try to conclude this unfortunate encounter on some note of tolerable amenity. 'But I beg your pardon,' he said. 'Only you wouldn't, would you, think to treat your own children in that fashion?'

'God damn it, sir, I'd touch up my own boy from time to time on due occasion given – supposing I had a boy, that is. Nothing but womenfolk in my house, curse it. A wife and three daughters, sir! Admirable, all of them. Delightful in every way. But the bloody place is Petticoat Hall, all the same.'

Honeybath was not quite sure how to receive this extraordinary communication. It revealed, he reflected, a morbidity precisely opposite to that attributable to Francis Kilvert, who had been for petticoats all the time, and the younger the better. In an odd way he was beginning to find Sylvanus Wyndowe, the Mullion roarer, not unattractive. If he had a tendency to make culpable assignations with rustic wenches in barns, it was perhaps prompted by a dumb desire to provide himself with a belated male issue even on the wrong side of the blanket – or the tump of hay. This, although undeniably flagitious, was something human in its way. Sylvanus, as a younger brother, had presumably no broad acres to be inherited. But his sense of the grievousness of being denied a son and heir was demonstrably genuine and burdensome, all the same. Honeybath, in fact, felt for him, and wished that their first encounter had not been of so signally unfortunate a character.

'I think,' he said, 'that you must be Mr Sylvanus Wyndowe? If so, perhaps I may be permitted to introduce myself, as I am at present your brother's guest. Henry and I were schoolfellows. My name is Charles Honeybath.'

'My dear Sir Charles, I am absolutely delighted to meet you!' Sylvanus produced this as a shout, and at once shook hands with the enthusiasm of one who believes himself at last to have found a long-hoped-for boon companion.

'Not Sir Charles, Mr Wyndowe. Plain Mr Honeybath.'

'Good God!' Sylvanus appeared appalled. 'Crooners and footballers and low comedians honoured on every hand, and fellows eminent in literature and the arts and so forth ignored. It must distress the Queen very much. But what can the poor lady do? Has nothing at all in her own pocket, they say. Shocking times, Mr Honeybath. Bloody awful times, in fact.'

Honeybath, although he doubted the validity of at least some of these propositions, was rather gratified by such enthusiasm from an unexpected quarter. He also felt instructed, although not exactly edified, by the manner in which any element of embarrassment inherent in the initial phase of this encounter had been cast into oblivion in his new acquaintance's mind. It was now possible to advance upon a little civil conversation about the proposed portrait of Lady Mullion – in the course of which Sylvanus Wyndowe did not hesitate to avow that he had been a strong proponent of the idea in the first place, and indeed of his having been convinced that Honeybath was the ideal choice for the job. He had been much impressed by Honeybath's treatment – particularly of the horse – in a recent effort commemorating the long services to fox hunting of a fellow MFH in the next county. If he had a bean of his own, he said, or could whip up a sufficient number of chums prepared to come forward with the ready, he would be on Honeybath's doorstep any day himself – and damned-well leading one of his own nags by the bridle.

Having delivered himself of this fond thought, Mr Wyndowe was prompted to glance at his watch – and to announce (with the first hint of perturbation he had betrayed during this peculiar meeting) that if he didn't stir his stumps he would be late for the trough, which was something his wife and daughters particularly disapproved of. But at least he would have the pleasure of seeing Honeybath again soon, since it was his intention to drop into the castle with his family sometime within the next few days.

With this encouraging thought, Sylvanus again shook hands vigorously, and then walked off hurriedly in what was presumably the direction of the Mullion dower house. Honeybath, remembering the black tie, hurried too.

9

It was the custom at the castle that Lord Wyndowe, destined to be Earl of Mullion, should yank Great-aunt Camilla out of her lift on those occasions when she elected to dine with the family. 'Yank' was Cyprian's own word, and expressed the fact that he took a dark view of the whole thing. This was in the first instance because Miss Wyndowe herself took a dark view of any public and sanctioned indulgence in preprandial drinks. The serving of cocktails or even of a glass of sherry in a drawing-room at such an hour was, she believed, a disagreeable practice recently brought into vogue among commercial people. What gentlemen did in more appropriate apartments was their own affair, and Cyprian could no doubt demand gin in Savine's pantry just as in former years he had been accustomed to demand chocolate biscuits and ginger pop in the housekeeper's room. She was not disposed to be censorious in such matters. But decanters on a drawing-room table constituted a very vulgar idea indeed.

Cyprian, owning a somewhat divided nature, was unable to let his conduct on these occasions match his familiar speech. He received his Great-aunt Camilla (not that she was exactly that) with unvarying gravity, and the 'yanking' resolved itself into offering her his arm with a decorum which would have been wholly adequate to the demands of the strictest Victorian society.

Whether the arm was necessary other than as a matter of form Honeybath, observing the ritual for the first time, felt unable to determine. Miss Wyndowe was an old woman, and she looked older than she was – a fact to be attributed, perhaps, to the stresses and strains of intermittent nervous disturbance. She could certainly move at will under her own steam, with no more assistance than that of a stout but elegant ebony and silver walking-stick. At the bottom of the lift, however, there was held in reserve for her more ambitious perambulations that sort of multipedous device which, cautiously advanced in front of aged persons, falsifies the ancient gnomic assertion that as we begin our life on four feet so must we end it on only three. The lift had clearly been installed specifically for her use, since her quarters were almost as elevated as the castle's great tower – from which Prince Rupert was reputed to have observed and directed sundry operations of war. Miss Wyndowe looked as if she would be capable of something of the sort herself; she had been a handsome woman, and had a commanding presence still. In just what her independent establishment consisted it wasn't given to Honeybath to discover. But he suspected that she was one who could not prudently be left for long to her own devices. It seemed wholly amiable in the Mullions to incorporate this not particularly close kinswoman in their household, even if it was on what was coming to be known as the granny-flat principle.

Lord Wyndowe continued his wardenship of the old lady on the way to the dining-room. There, at his mother's direction, he led her to a chair which proved to be on Honeybath's right hand. As her prescriptive place on family occasions would presumably be next to Lord Mullion, this arrangement appeared to suggest that Honeybath was, as it were, to be pitched in at the deep end without delay, and cope as he could with whatever mild or not so mild eccentricities it was Miss Wyndowe's habit to display. Honeybath had, of course, already been presented to her, but as her only acknowledgement of the ceremony had been a grave bow he had no idea whether she had made anything either of his identity or the occasion of his presence at the castle. Thus established at table, and settled in her place by Savine with what Honeybath felt to be particular solicitousness and gloom, Miss Wyndowe reposed for some minutes in deep abstraction. Although Lady Mullion had at once begun to talk firmly to Patty on her left hand, Honeybath made no immediate attempt to initiate a conversation with his other neighbour. She was a member of the household, and he himself had never been near the place before, so the ball might be considered as in her court. Presently, indeed, she did turn her head and look at him. For some moments it was a calm and considering gaze, such as any woman habituated to good society would employ when determining the probable interests and resources of a stranger with whom talk must be carried on. Then her expression changed. It was as if she had detected Honeybath in slipping some of the Mullion spoons and forks into his pocket, or pierced a disguise and perceived that here was the burglar who had broken in upon her the night before – or even the escaped lethal lunatic lately mentioned in a local paper. And the effect was undeniably lunatic in itself. There was suddenly something quite wild about Miss Camilla Wyndowe. Honeybath didn't like it at all. He even felt considerably alarmed. His hosts, he told himself, might at least have spared him this all too sudden confrontation with something out of the cupboard.

'Have you got a good vicar here?' Miss Wyndowe asked. Her tone was as politely calm as her expression had been a minute before. And the question was one, on the instant, uncommonly difficult to reply to. Honeybath might, indeed, say with an answering calm something like, 'Dear lady, you're off your head.' But that, it had to be acknowledged, wouldn't do at all.

'Why, yes,' he said. 'I believe so. Dr Atlay, is it not? I had the pleasure of meeting him this morning, as a matter of fact.'

Miss Wyndowe frowned. She appeared to regard this response as fundamentally unsatisfactory. And in the brief silence that succeeded, Lady Mullion (who must have been more alert than she seemed to be) turned to her husband's kinswoman without haste. 'Camilla, dear,' she said, 'you forget that you are not on a visit. You are at home, you know. And there is Henry at the other end of the table.'

'At home? I am not a visitor in this house? How one's keenest perceptions betray one! I am confused, indeed.'

This extraordinary speech, Honeybath thought, might have been out of the kind of novel (at one time brought into vogue by Miss Ivy Compton-Burnett, whom he greatly admired) in which the numerous members of excessively well-bred families are excessively nasty to one another in an excessively oblique manner. But no such effect in fact attended Miss Wyndowe's words. They had been uttered dreamily and entirely without animus. And now, without pause, she turned back to Honeybath with an expression that had wholly returned to an agreeable calm.

'Have you seen any good plays lately?' she inquired. 'I have been told there is something quite amusing by Sir Arthur Wing Pinero. So odd a name! I believe the play to be called *The Gay Lord Quex*. It sounds as if it was about ducks. Sir Arthur, of course, is not so witty as Mr Wilde. But I am told *his* morals are exceptionable.'

'It's not at all improbable.' Honeybath felt that he now had his bearings with Miss Wyndowe. She lived in the past – and not even her own past, unless his chronology was badly astray. He had only to humour this foible – or debility – with a decent gravity and urbanity. 'I seldom go to the theatre nowadays,' he said. 'The actors are not what they were. Who now is so moving as Beerbohm Tree, or so amusing as Charles Hawtrey?'

'Or Little Titch,' Miss Wyndowe said with sudden animation. 'I adore Little Titch.'

'Yes, indeed.' It was rather feebly that Honeybath offered this concurrence, since it had occurred to him to wonder whether the alarming old woman was making fun of him. His embarrassment must have been remarked by Patty, since she now struck in promptly from the other side of the table.

'You do know, don't you, Aunt,' she asked, 'that Mr Honeybath, while at the castle, is going to paint my mother's portrait? Mr Honeybath is a Royal Academician, and his portraits are held in very high regard.' Patty paused, and must then have remembered one of Miss Wyndowe's more marked eccentricities. 'He is considered,' she added, 'quite the equal of either Mr Sargent or Sir John Lavery.'

'I am most delighted to hear it.' Miss Wyndowe said this with perfect propriety and ease of address. 'But Mr Sargent's work I do not myself greatly care for. More often than not, he paints people who are extremely common – or worse. He might be described as a kind of Velazquez *de la boue*. Nor do I think, Patty, that from the Americans in general we have much to learn. It is to be regretted, indeed, that the laying of the submarine cable has so expedited communication with them. Mr Honeybath, I am sure that you agree with me.'

Honeybath produced some sort of murmur. Great-aunt Camilla, it seemed to him, was not mad quite as most people who are mad are mad. She certainly retained powers of astringent judgement and pungent expression of it. He wondered whether, were he to have her squarely before him through a dozen sittings, he would arrive at some sense of knowing his way about her. But the mere thought of such an assignment was alarming. And it might perfectly easily have happened. Henry could simply have invited him down to paint the portrait of a distinguished elderly member of his family whom he desired to honour. The thought made Honeybath reflect once more on the hazardousness of his calling.

But now Miss Wyndowe (who seldom paused to eat) was well launched upon table-talk, mostly within the wide field of art and her own peregrinations in it. She had been received by Monet himself at Giverny, and had been a good deal encouraged by him. (Here at least, Honeybath thought, was a chronological possibility, if only because Monet had lived into his later eighties.) She had also wandered for some months in Provence, where the younger painters were beginning to congregate, and here too her budding talent had been freely acknowledged. She still owned numerous memorials of that time, and when she came to domesticate herself at Mullion her cousin Sylvanus (Henry's father, not to be confused with the person in the dower house) had been kind enough to hang some of her work in the castle. And there it still was, although she didn't, for the moment, precisely recall its location. After dinner, however, she would require that Honeybath be conducted to it.

Honeybath, who was not infrequently called upon to admire the productions of talented amateurs, expressed his keen anticipation of this pleasure, and cautiously refrained from regretting Miss Wyndowe's apparent neglect of the thraldom of artistic labour over some four or five subsequent decades. Miss Wyndowe's reminiscences, although perhaps not untouched by imagination and certainly somewhat egocentric in effect, seemed sane enough in their way. She was undoubtedly dotty, all the same, and perhaps it was an early onset of this unfortunate condition that had dried up in her the well-springs of creation. Honeybath knew other artists to whom this had happened: inheritors, it might be said, of unfulfilled renown.

'But you didn't' – it occurred to him to ask, recalling Lady Mullion's account of the matter – 'think to go on to Italy?'

'Most certainly not!' This was snapped out by Miss Wyndowe with so sudden a vehemence that Honeybath was startled. He had thoughtlessly stumbled, he supposed, on the dangerous territory of the old lady's religious fanaticism.

'Or ever thought,' he continued hastily, 'to travel in the Far East? I have myself always regretted never having visited Japan.'

'Japan? Decidedly not! The sanitary conditions there are certain to be deplorable. And that held of Italy, at least at that time. My maid, Pipton, who accompanied me in France, had been briefly in Italy with my cousin, Parthenope Wyndowe. The conditions, Pipton said, were atrocious, and such as we should not think to face. And *that*, Mr Honeybath, was the occasion of my not venturing further than Provence.'

'It was very prudent, no doubt.' These bizarre considerations, he reflected, seemed to have little to do with a maniacal disapproval of the so-called Bishop of Rome. But Miss Wyndowe was really a muddled old soul, although in some ways she had to be regarded as sharp enough. It certainly wouldn't do to challenge her on minor inconsistencies revealed in these autobiographical ramblings. So he cast round for a radical change of subject which should take him, as it were, to the end of his innings with Great-aunt Camilla. Some more sustained attention on the part of his hostess seemed to him a little overdue. Perhaps she was acting on the assumption that her aged kinswoman would particularly enjoy a long colloquy with a fellow artist.

'This part of the country,' he said, 'always seems to me particularly beautiful at the present time of year. I had a delightful drive down this morning, on secondary roads for the most part. One sees much more of one's surroundings that way.'

'Is that why you were late for luncheon at the castle?'

'Well, no.' Honeybath was a shade disconcerted that Miss Wyndowe should have been told about his small failure as a punctilious guest, and suspected that her informant had been young Cyprian, who might even have adorned his tale with a little ludicrous fiction. 'What happened was that I ran out of petrol. Or, rather, I imagined I had.'

'Imagined you had? How very peculiar!'

'It does sound odd.' Honeybath considered embarking on a description of little green and red lights, but reflected that such gadgets didn't belong to Miss Wyndowe's period. 'However, I was rescued by one of Henry's gardeners, an obliging lad called Swithin Gore.' Swithin, as one whom he had unjustly aspersed, was still running in Honeybath's head.

'Gore? I don't think I know him.' Miss Wyndowe appeared to consider this remark with care. 'But he may be the boy who used to look after my donkey-cart, and who has received some promotion since then. Do you use a donkey cart, Mr Honeybath? As you know, the Queen enjoys driving one. Only they call hers a donkey carriage.'

'Is that so?' This information struck Honeybath as improbable, until it occurred to him that the sovereign thus augustly invoked had probably enjoyed this mode of conveyance at Osborne or Balmoral rather a long time ago.

'And – now I come to think of it – there have been Gores on the estate over a number of generations. I seem to recall an Abel Gore. One might imagine him to have been some sort of bull.'

'The boy who coped with my car wasn't at all like a bull.' It had taken Honeybath a moment to catch up with the sense of Miss

Wyndowe's remark, which revealed a process of mind as peculiar as had yet come from her. He wondered whether she was adept at advanced crossword puzzles. 'As a matter of fact, when I first glanced at him I supposed he might be Cyprian. But that had something to do with what he happened to be carrying.'

'And also an Ammon Gore.' Miss Wyndowe was pursuing her own line of thought. 'Or was it Mammon? The lower classes were formerly prone to make an uninstructed use of scriptural names. But I think it was Ammon. The Ammonites were the children of Lot. His wife, you will recall, was of a retrospective habit, and was turned into a pillar of salt as a result. The notion of a pillar of salt is elusive, but some sort of stalagmite may have given rise to the conception. Can you tell me, Mr Honeybath, whether there are stalagmites in the Holy Land? It is on record as flowing with milk and honey – but not, so far as I know, with carbonate of lime.'

Honeybath felt that this was getting beyond him. He wondered whether it represented a form of witty conversation fashionable at dinner-tables in this aged person's youth. Or was it some kind of family joke that hadn't been explained to him? This last speculation, which really had very little sense to it, at least confirmed the fact that he had a strong impulse to be bewildered by Great-aunt Camilla. He remembered Lady Mullion's saying, on an impulse, that she felt her husband's kinswoman as suggesting that some mystery attached to her; that she had a secret. Might it be that at least she had a past – which was not quite the same idea, but came close to it? The oddity of her conversation seemed not entirely a matter of senility or mental decay. It had too much intermittent point to it for that. Was it, conceivably, in part a defensive mechanism; something left over from a period in which an evasive inconsequence was useful to her? This notion, if not without subtlety, was rather unpersuasive as well, and Honeybath abandoned such idle speculation. During the rest of dinner he talked in the main with Lady Mullion. But on several occasions when conversation among the small party grew more general, and Miss Wyndowe contributed to it with a kind of random liberality, it struck him that a good deal of the effect she created proceeded from nothing more remarkable than a singularly patchy memory. This seemed to hold alike over the near and the remote past. If her memory was to be regarded as a route-map of the large areas of experience she had traversed in her eighty years (or whatever exactly they might be) then there were blank spaces scattered indifferently all over it. This, of course, was a rash conclusion to think to arrive at with any confidence on so short an acquaintance with the old creature as his at present was. Her mind might well reveal more extravagant contours on a better knowledge of her. Indeed, he had been as good as warned that it was so. But at least she was far from boring. Honeybath caught himself as being almost sorry, after all, that he hadn't been invited to set up his easel in front of her.

10

The four ladies had withdrawn, and the three gentlemen had addressed themselves to a second glass of port, when the dining-room door opened and Dr Atlay appeared. He was received by Lord Mullion cordially but in so entirely casual a manner that it was clear he was treated virtually as a member of the household, coming and going as he pleased. Lady Mullion had, indeed, mentioned to Honeybath that the vicar, who had various antiquarian interests, from time to time pursued his researches in the castle library. Perhaps he had been doing this now, or perhaps he had merely dropped in to deliver the parish magazine. His having gravitated in the direction he now had, however, suggested that he was not without the thought of material recruitment in his mind, and after accepting port he accepted a cigar as well. No doubt he had devoted a long day to pastoral cares, and was glad to become much a man of leisure at this late evening hour.

'I have paid my respects in the drawing-room,' he said, 'and gather, Mr Honeybath, that you have made an early grand tour of the castle.'

'Lady Mullion was good enough to do me a kind of private view.'

'I am delighted to hear it. There is much to remark, is there not?'

'Armour rusting in his halls On the blood of Mullion calls,' Cyprian said, reaching for a decanter. Cyprian, who at Cambridge regularly devoted two or three hours a week to his studies in English literature, was fond of coming forward with this sort of thing. 'Not that the stuff does rust. A chap comes down from London twice a year and burnishes it and lacquers it so that you'd think we kept a staff of armourers in the dungeons. All part of the show.'

'I imagine,' Dr Atlay said, 'that your guest was more interested in some of the less martial exhibits. The Zoffanys come to mind. You have seen them, Mr Honeybath?'

'Not yet. There is a great deal to see, as you have remarked.'

'There have been nabob Wyndowes, and Zoffany went to work on them in India. And then there are the Hilliards. I recall your mentioning that you would be interested in them.'

'Yes, indeed. Lady Mullion pointed them out to me in passing, but we didn't pause on them.'

'Take a dekko at them now, eh?' Lord Mullion said, rising. 'Jolly little things, I've always thought, and uncommonly valuable, they say. Have to keep them in the library now, under lock and key and so forth. So come along, all of you.'

'Excellent!' Dr Atlay said. 'It's some time since I took a look at them. And it's longer still, I imagine, since Wyndowe did. Do you good, Wyndowe. It cannot be maintained that you are too well up on your ancestors.'

Cyprian got to his feet, scowling – perhaps because the idea bored him, or perhaps because he disliked being addressed in the vicar's semi-formal manner.

So the gentlemen moved off in a body through the castle – Honeybath willingly enough, although he would perhaps have preferred to make the acquaintance of three unfamiliar Hilliards (and defunct Wyndowes) in more instructed company. At the library door they encountered Savine, who looked at them reproachfully. At the castle, after-dinner coffee was taken in the drawing-room. Perhaps Savine felt that it was growing cold there – or perhaps that the prescriptive interval had already passed beyond which the ladies ought not to be left to their own devices.

'Reliable man, Savine,' Lord Mullion said to Honeybath when the door had closed behind him. 'Strong on security, and keeps everything under his own hand. He's a great comfort to us all – eh, Cyprian?'

'Regular nannie,' Cyprian said sulkily. 'He keeps a damned sight too much of an eye on things, if you ask me. If I drop into his pantry for something, he bloody well makes me feel I ought to be signing for it as if in some rotten club.'

As by 'something' it was to be suspected that Lord Wyndowe meant whisky or brandy, this small demonstration a little lacked edification. His father, however, was, as usual, unruffled by what he no doubt regarded still as mere adolescent gracelessness. Being an heir in a place like this, Honeybath thought, must have its irritations and be conducive to mild frictions. Boosie as a rebel was more attractive than her brother.

The library was a lofty and enormous room, none too well-lit at any time, and surely uncommonly chilly for much of the year. But Lord Mullion looked round it with complacency.

'Martin moles around here a great deal,' he said to Honeybath. 'Martin' was the Reverend Dr Atlay. 'Turned up a good deal of soil lately, Martin – and the family skeletons along with it?' Lord Mullion invited innocent laughter at this pleasantry, but it appeared to take the vicar a little aback.

'There is work in progress, my dear Mullion,' he said. 'That is how a scholar would express the matter. And where family papers are abundant one never knows what one may turn up next. But I shall think twice before disinterring any skeletons. It is a disagreeable operation even in a churchyard. I should certainly not wish to undertake it rashly in a library.'

'But what about making dry bones live, eh?' It appeared to be with some further whimsical intention that Lord Mullion produced this biblical reference. 'Plenty of theology,' he continued, as if continuing this process of associative thinking. 'But I've never much looked at it. I'll leave that to Cyprian, when he decides to take holy orders. It's a long time since an Earl of Mullion turned himself into a bishop as well. He might begin as your curate, Martin. Lowest rung of the ladder, you know. Learn the job from the bottom, like lads the business chaps perch on high stools in their counting-houses. Think it over, Cyprian.'

Cyprian produced another of his scowls, for which Honeybath didn't altogether blame him. The future owner of Castle Mullion clad in purple and lawn was as bizarre a notion as the archaic one of young gentlemen of less distinguished lineage perched in front of ledgers. Henry was a man of temperate habit (probably unlike his brother Sylvanus) but inclined, it seemed, to gamesomeness after his couple of glasses of port. He had also turned a little vague, and for a moment even seemed disorientated in his own library.

'Let me see,' he said. 'I rather think – '

'In the window embrasure, my dear Mullion.' Dr Atlay had taken his host by the arm. 'The showcase with the velvet cover, you know. The cover is to ward off any direct rays from the sun.'

'To be sure – and here the little chaps are.' Lord Mullion had whisked away the cover indicated to him. 'Wonderful things in their way, and I can't think how the fellow managed them. Paintbrushes like needles, he must have had. And the result, I don't doubt, as authentic as the latest tiptop colour photography. But artistically in another street, of course.'

'As a consequence of which,' Cyprian said, 'they'd fetch rather more than the family photograph album, or even the entire *oeuvre* of Great-aunt Camilla.'

'Perfectly true, my dear boy.' Lord Mullion had the air of treating this as a penetrating observation. 'And another thing, you know. They're painted on chicken-skin. Odd use for the stuff.'

'Not these,' Dr Atlay said. 'As Honeybath could tell us, chicken-skin came later. Thin vellum mounted on card, if I remember aright. There is probably an account of the technique in Hilliard's *Arte of Limning*, written round about 1600. Would that be correct, Honeybath?'

'I don't know about the date, but it has wonderful passages on the psychology of portraiture.' Honeybath was studying the miniatures, which were only imperfectly revealed within their fastness, with a good deal of attention. 'Are they all identified?'

'The lady on the left,' Atlay said, 'is Lady Lucy Wyndowe, who was reckoned a great beauty in her time. In the middle is the third earl.

71

The young man on the right we can't pin down. I have always thought he rather resembles the *Young Man in Deep Mourning* in the Portland Collection, which is a very late work of Hilliard's indeed. Remark the masterly effect of evanescence in the youth's smile, as if he had been momentarily diverted from serious thought.'

This sensitive observation was respectfully received, and Honeybath peered more closely. Lord Mullion noticed this.

'Get them out, eh?' he said. 'Just hold on. The key is with the plate, and so forth, in Savine's safe.'

'Honeybath's closer inspection might better take place in daylight, and on a later occasion,' Dr Atlay said. 'And I am reminded that there is a hint of impatience in the drawing-room, at least on Miss Wyndowe's part. She doesn't precisely aim to display what Wyndowe calls her *oeuvre*. But it appears that several of her watercolours are hung somewhere in the castle, and she has taken it into her head, my dear Honeybath, that you should be conducted to them and, no doubt, offer an opinion on their merits. We can be confident that you can do that sort of thing very well.'

'Ah, yes.' Honeybath had to make an effort to attend to this, for other matters were on his mind. Nor did he much care for the tone of urbane patronage in the vicar's last remark. 'Miss Wyndowe did mention something of the kind to me.'

'Then we'd better cut along,' Lord Mullion said. The circumspect thing at the castle, one felt, was to attend promptly to Great-aunt Camilla's whims while she was in circulation. 'We can have a go at these little jossers another time. And I've remembered about the vellum. Stuck on playing-cards, they say. Old ones, it seems. Economical trick.'

On this sober thought Lord Mullion led the way out of the library. Honeybath remained silent, and for the very good reason that for some minutes he had been uncertain whether to speak or not. The astonishing fact was that he suddenly found himself in a position of extreme delicacy. Lady Lucy Wyndowe was all right. The second earl was all right. But the miniature resembling the *Young Man in Deep Mourning* was all wrong. Honeybath had enjoyed no more than a glimpse of it. His sense of such matters, however, was by native endowment and long training almost preternaturally acute. He had realized instantly that what was on display within that little frame was an excellent reproduction of a Jacobean miniature and not an original. It wasn't even a replica. It belonged, in fact, to that art of colour photography which Lord Mullion had so lately commended.

It was in some desperation that Honeybath, on the way to join the ladies, chewed over this discovery. There came into his head Cyprian's facetious remark about pawning the Mullion diamonds. Was it some rather similar activity that he had stumbled upon? He remembered a celebrated case in which professional thieves had successfully brought off a similar trick – and actually with a substantial oil painting. The substituted print had hung undetected for weeks or months in a great house owned by persons even more uninstructed in artistic matters than the Wyndowes, and by the time a competent eye had fallen upon it the original had passed securely into the possession of an unscrupulous collector. Something of the kind might well have happened here, and much less detectably with a minute object like an extremely valuable miniature. On the other hand there was the uncomfortable possibility that the theft (for it could scarcely be called other than that) had been what is known as an inside job. Honeybath was in a difficult moral position.

It seemed to be his duty to communicate his awkward discovery to Henry at once – or almost at once, since it was certainly an occasion for the utmost confidentiality. But what if Henry himself was at the bottom of the thing? This staggering thought almost made Honeybath halt in his tracks. Had Henry been raising the wind in a quiet way – perhaps to meet some liability which he didn't want to reveal to his family? If this were so – and presuming Lord Mullion to be the undisputed owner of the Hilliards, which was by no means certain – nothing positively criminal would, after all, be involved, and it wouldn't be for Honeybath himself to meddle with his friend's secret. But the idea was, of course, preposterous. The innocence of Lord Mullion – his innocence in every sense – was just not open to question. And he certainly wasn't the kind of actor who could have pulled off a wholly deceptive part during the past quarter of an hour.

So what about Cyprian, who was very much the sort of young man one might suspect of a precocious ability to run into considerable debt? Whether Cyprian was clever or not, Honeybath didn't know. He was presumably one of nature's non-starters on the intellectual side of Cambridge academic life. But that told one nothing at all; Honeybath knew that inexpugnably idle undergraduates often pack a great deal of ability behind a deceptive façade. It would be extremely sad if Cyprian were to prove to have been behaving with scandalous dishonesty in his own home.

Then there was Dr Atlay, who knew a good deal about artistic matters and was fond of advertising the fact. Atlay seemed to have the run of the castle, and particularly of the library. And hadn't he been a shade keen to cut short the inspection of the Hilliards? It was true that it was he who had referred to Honeybath's probable interest in them in the first place. But hadn't he ensured thereby that he would be present and in a position to control the situation as he had in fact done?

That the ladies of the household were involved – so Honeybath told himself – was a suspicion too fantastic to be entertained. Yet he was a little inclined to wonder about Lady Patience Wyndowe – Patty, as he had come to think of her. Patty didn't say much, but Honeybath had come to feel that there was something she was brooding over, and that this, whatever it was, had a character in some mysterious way requiring concealment from the rest of her family. Was it Patty who had a guilty secret? Honeybath was seriously entertaining this nebulous notion when something quite different started up in his mind. *What about that man Savine?* Honeybath, although his own family background was such that it had been quite natural that young Henry Wyndowe should be his fag, had never himself enjoyed the services of a butler; nor had his father done so. He regarded upper menservants as rather a sinister crowd. It was no doubt customary that your butler should have the wardenship of your silver in quite a big way, but it seemed mildly dotty to hand over to him the wardenship of three miniatures by Nicholas Hilliard. There had been a time within living memory when such things were scarcely regarded as significant works of art. But they must be uncommonly valuable now.

Thus did Charles Honeybath, much like a detective in the latter part of a mystery story, turn hither and thither the swift mind (as Homer says) while surveying a field full of suspects. It will be remarked that he had rejected Lady Mullion for the role, and pretty well forgotten her younger daughter, the schoolgirl Boosie. But as the present chronicle, being veridical, enjoys all the unpredictability of history, it would be rash to base any hypothesis upon this circumstance.

They had joined the ladies, who were engaged, in the distinctly grand drawing-room of Mullion Castle, in the unassuming activity of watching the nine o'clock news. The television set, indeed, peeped reticently out of a cupboard and could be banished behind a door in elegant linen-fold panelling, Lord Mullion having been advised that the exposure of such an object would militate against the Wednesday and Saturday visitors' persuasion that they were in the presence of only the very highest sort of gracious living. Lady Mullion switched off the set at once.

'Nothing but minor fatalities,' she said briskly. 'Motor coaches tumbling into yawning chasms. Fortunately there is nothing of the sort in the park, or we might be in trouble tomorrow. And in Nottingham a dog has been badly bitten by its demented owner. That young man with the spotty face hastened to the scene "to report" as they say. Only the dog was already in hospital. Charles, please help yourself to coffee.'

Honeybath obeyed, not without a lurking feeling that he could have done with brandy as well, an indulgence which the continued presence of Miss Wyndowe presumably forbade. But perhaps when she had been yanked into her lift again there would be whisky before going to bed.

The *oeuvre* immediately came under discussion, but there was fortunately no proposal that it should be at once exhibited *in toto*. In her own apartments Miss Wyndowe kept several portfolios of her drawings and watercolours, and these Mr Honeybath was to have the privilege of turning over on some convenient occasion when he took tea with her. At the moment the problem was to locate those actually hanging somewhere in the castle. Everybody was vague about this in a manner that scarcely suggested any lively regard for Great-aunt Camilla's work. It was felt that one of the twice-weekly ladies (by which was meant Lord Mullion's locally recruited guides) would know, and that most probably it would be Miss Kinder-Scout, who had made the pictures her special study. And then Cyprian came up with the suggestion that the elusive paintings might 'be among the fish and things in that kitchen corridor'. This was perhaps awkwardly expressed, but nobody seemed embarrassed by it; nor did Miss Wyndowe herself evince any disapprobation at the idea. Honeybath felt at sea about the fish (which could scarcely be at sea themselves) and wondered whether, in the macabre fashion sometimes to be remarked in restaurants, the Mullion kitchens ran to aquarium-like receptacles in which there swam, in blissful ignorance of their fate, the second course in tomorrow's dinner.

The fish proved to inhabit individual glass cases, and to be stuffed. But did one stuff fish? Was such a branch of taxidermy feasible? Honeybath had often wondered, and never found out. Perhaps the fish in their glass cases were faithful replicas, executed in plaster or wax, of actual fish which had fallen to the skill of angling Wyndowes long ago. There was conceivably a special branch of sculpture devoted to such creation, or it might simply be a side-line profitably pursued by the skilled assistants of Madame Tussaud.

These were absurd speculations, such as ought not to have deflected Honeybath either from further perpending his late anxieties or from exhibiting a civil zeal in the hunt for Great-aunt Camilla's pictures. His companions, however, now felt that they were hot on the scent. The kitchen corridor was a broad, stone-flagged thoroughfare, and followed a gentle curve which must have been dictated by one of the external walls of the castle. On one side hung the fish. On the other, frame hard against frame in the fashion favoured by collectors long ago, hung hundreds rather than scores of small pictures of the most various sort. Sporting prints predominated, but there was no end of portrait heads, architectural and topographical sketches, stormy seascapes, an aphrodisiac nudes, the offerings of laborious schoolchildren in the way of painfully 'shaded' cylinders and cubes, woolly alphabets and nebulous scriptural scenes executed in embroidery by persons in the same defenceless phase of life, illuminated testimonials of respect and esteem from well-affected tenants and their wretched labourers, royal warrants and commissions appointing sundry loyal subjects (styled 'cousins' for the nonce) to do this or that round about the empire, rent-rolls and dairy-books and cellar-books, fragments of which had struck some earlier Lord Mullion as being of keen antiquarian or historical interest. A catalogue of all this could have been almost indefinitely prolonged, and the only common denominator that could be extracted from the lot was that of mediocrity or near-mediocrity. Here and there it might have been possible to pick out the equivalent of Cyprian's piece of Chinese porcelain lurking in a potting shed. Honeybath, for example, believed himself to have briefly glimpsed a representation in oils of an obstinately static horse-race which might have been by John, or by John F, or by John N Sartorius, and which might conceivably be flogged to an artistically minded Emir or Sheik for several hundred (or even thousand) pounds. But the total effect was not inspiring, and it could hardly be supposed that Miss Wyndowe would be too pleased to find the labours of her brush or pencil jostling in such company.

This thought appeared to occur to Lord Mullion.

'Fascinating part of the place, this,' he said heartily. 'They all come along here, you know – the visiting crowd, I mean – on their way to the kitchen. The kitchen is supposed to be a great feature of the castle, being so extremely medieval and so forth with all those spits and ovens and tables made out of entire oak trees and the like. But our clients can scarcely be dragged away from the corridor. Bella Kinder-Scout was remarking on the fact to me only the other day.'

Great-aunt Camilla seemed unimpressed by this, or indeed by anything else. She had made her way down the corridor assisted by both Cyprian and her multipedous device. She looked, or was contriving to look, extremely tired – which was a state in which her quite dippy component seemed likely to gain the ascendant. In this condition she was liable to say anything under the sun. Honeybath felt that the present expedition had been sadly misconceived. His own attention wandered back to the stuffed or sculptured fish, which were at least not wholly remote from Nature's family. He remarked the interesting fact that they were nearly all positioned in the same way, facing from left to right as one looked at them. This is the artist's immemorial resource for setting his creations within the tide of time: face to the right and you are moving into the future; turn your head and you are glancing back into the past. It is a psychologically obscure but nevertheless powerful symbolism, and Honeybath was meditating upon it in a professional manner when he was arrested by a sudden shout from Lord Wyndowe. The moment was one, although he had no notion of the fact, pregnant for the future of the Wyndowe family.

'Here they are!'

Cyprian's voice rang down the corridor. Just so might his uncle, Sylvanus Wyndowe, have bellowed 'Gone away!' or something of the sort in the hunting field, and it would almost have been appropriate if the whole little company had broken briskly into a canter. And indeed, as Honeybath was subsequently to reflect, the shout was to prove much like one initiating a rapid course of things leading from a view to a death in the morning.

But the actual quarry was far from exciting. Hanging between a dish of flabby fruit rendered in inexpertly handled oils and the charcoal head of somebody's favourite hound were two small watercolours each of which coped valiantly if unsuccessfully with outdoor scenes of a rather elaborate sort. And Miss Wyndowe had hobbled up and was pointing dramatically at the first of them.

'Ah,' she cried, 'dear, *dear* Azay-le-Rideau! Howl remember struggling with that fountain. But I was rewarded. Monet himself approved.'

Honeybath glanced at the picture. He more than glanced at the fountain. And then – cautiously – he glanced swiftly at Lord and Lady Mullion, at the girls, at Cyprian, at Dr Atlay. Perhaps they were gratified by the old lady's sudden animation, or perhaps they were bored. But certainly detectable in them was that curious quality of inattention so often to be remarked in people 'doing' overwhelming public galleries. The kitchen corridor wasn't exactly that. Its mere petty multitudinousness was wearisome, all the same.

'But surely –' Honeybath began, and broke off on detecting the note of irritation in his own voice. 'But surely,' he managed to say, 'the other picture was even more taxing, Miss Wyndowe? To get the glint of the water beneath –'

'Ah, but indeed! That bridge over the Seine at Argenteuil: it was daunting to attempt such a subject in the very steps of the Master himself. You remember his painting, Mr Honeybath?'

Honeybath certainly remembered Monet's painting: remembered the boldness of the bridge's span emphasized by the sickle of sky beneath, softened by the flutter of bunting above. But for the first time Great-aunt Camilla had embarrassed and even alarmed him. She *was* quite, quite mad. No woman in her senses could site Bernini's *Fontana del Bicchierone* somewhere on the Loire, or confound an affair of cast-iron girders with Ammanati's *Ponte a S. Trinità*.

Various civil remarks were made – and some of them by Honeybath to the best of his ability. He continued to find himself curiously put out. Something quite unaccountable and absurd had just happened; and it had happened hard upon something else which, if not absurd, was very unaccountable indeed. He had a dim sense that these two unaccountabilities were related, although he couldn't conceive how this might be so. The problem so preoccupied him that he had very little sense of the brief remaining events of the evening, which indeed chiefly consisted in getting Miss Wyndowe back into her lift. Eventually he found himself alone for a few minutes with Lord Mullion and (blessedly) a decanter of whisky. And it seemed to him there was nothing for it but to speak out.

'Do you know, Henry,' he began cautiously, 'that I think Miss Wyndowe must be mistaken in her impression that she never travelled in Italy?'

'My dear Charles, whatever do you mean?' Quite abruptly, Lord Mullion had put down his glass and was staring at his old schoolfellow in astonishment.

'Those two watercolours have nothing whatever to do with the places she mentioned – and which are, of course, both in France. The one is of a famous fountain at Tivoli, and the other is of an equally famous bridge in Florence.'

'God bless my soul! How very odd. But of course Great-aunt Camilla imagines things. Not a doubt about that.'

'But, as I understand the matter, it is quite firm family history, or persuasion, and has been for a long time, that on her Grand Tour as a young woman – for I suppose it may be called that – she firmly refused to enter Italy. Perhaps because she disliked the Pope, or perhaps because she distrusted the drains. If those two watercolour sketches are hers, then that record is nonsense.'

'Well, yes.' Lord Mullion had recourse to his glass, and appeared to find wisdom in it. 'They must be by somebody else, and she has it muddled up.'

'It's certainly a possibility.'

'A probability, I'd say. Remember the state of her mind.'

'I do remember it. But she is uncommonly positive – isn't she? – that she painted the things herself. And I believe the point could be proved or disproved through a little close comparative study of those two efforts with others that are undoubtedly her own work.'

'You don't say so?' Lord Mullion was impressed. 'But – do you know? She probably did the things from picture postcards or something like that. I did it myself as a kid.'

'It's another possibility.' Honeybath paused on this, and finished his whisky. It was on the tip of his tongue to say, 'And there's another thing', and to go on to tell Henry that he was at present the owner not of three but only of two miniatures by Nicholas Hilliard. But he refrained. He refrained because of a certain very odd idea which was beginning to harbour in his head. It was an idea of the kind that needs sleeping upon – and in all probability then needs burying.

'Not a doubt of it,' Lord Mullion was saying easily. 'The truth is you never know where you are with the old girl. We've got used to it, you know, and don't much bother ourselves about small mysteries. Clever of you to spot the thing, Charles. Never have spotted it myself. Martin Atlay might, being interested in that kind of thing. By the way, we'd better not challenge Camilla herself on the point. It might upset her. And then she can be very awkward indeed.'

'My dear Henry, I'd be speaking quite out of turn to her if I raised the question.' Honeybath hesitated. 'But I believe it may be worth thinking about, all the same.'

'Yes, of course. I quite agree with you.' Lord Mullion nodded sagely and vaguely, and one might readily have concluded that he would never give the matter another thought. 'Better get off to bed,' he said as he stood up. 'I do hope you'll sleep well, Charles. It's quiet enough here – if you don't mind the owls.'

11

It may have been an owl that awakened Honeybath in the small hours, but what he awoke to was a ghost. The ghost – which like many ghosts might have been no more than a perambulating scarecrow in a white sheet – was standing silently in a corner of the bedroom, in which the only illumination was from a faint moonlight. There was no reason to suppose that the ghost had uttered, moaned, or clanked a chain: its effect was of one waiting considerately to be taken notice of. Honeybath was not alarmed or even surprised, and he might thus be said to be conforming to the customary behaviour of persons encountering veridical apparitions as distinct from the story-book variety. Honeybath, in fact, got briskly out of bed.

'Can I do anything for you?' he asked politely.

At this the ghost did move, and did produce a sound. It turned and walked slowly towards the door to the accompaniment of a faint tap-tapping on the polished floor. It opened the door (which is a much more difficult feat for a ghost than merely vanishing through a solid wall), passed out of the bedroom, and closed the door behind it. Then the tap-tapping receded down the corridor.

A brief irresolution now possessed Honeybath. Although his privacy had been invaded, and his just repose disturbed, it was really no business of his. There was no doubt in his mind that he had simply witnessed something already described to him: untoward nocturnal behaviour on the part of Miss Camilla Wyndowe. Whether somnambulistically or otherwise, the old lady was prone to these wanderings around Mullion Castle – and apparently with a degree of mobility scarcely commanded by her on other occasions. He couldn't recall that Lady Mullion had recorded herself as taking any action during the similar incident she had described to him, so he had no clue as to what, if anything, he should himself do. It was hard to believe that this aged and crazed person was allowed thus to wander at will, or that she was doing so now other than because, thus in the middle of the night, she had eluded the care of whatever nurse or similar attendant had the duty of looking after her. She had been without torch or candle, and although she presumably knew the castle well it could not be anything except a singularly dangerous place to wander about in after such a fashion. It would be irresponsible not to follow her at once, and keep an eye on her till he could somehow summon help.

Honeybath, unfortunately, had neither torch nor candle either – and not even a box of matches. Unlike Miss Wyndowe, he was totally unfamiliar with the lay-out of the castle, vague about which way to turn as soon as he left his room, totally unaware of where anybody else was sleeping. So he must catch up with the old lady before she disappeared from view, and keep her in sight until he could decide how, with least fuss, to alert one or another member of the household.

These thoughts had taken him out of his bedroom and into the corridor. There was fortunately a gleam of moonlight here as well, but it afforded no glimpse of Miss Wyndowe. It looked as if there was nothing for it but move about knocking on doors at random until he found a tenanted one and could report on the situation. But now, half-way down the corridor, another door opened and Miss Wyndowe emerged through it. She shut it softly behind her, crossed the corridor to another door, appeared to listen intently for a moment, and then disappeared into this further room. It occurred to Honeybath that she was simply engaged in the bizarre ritual of making a round of the castle and satisfying herself that all its inmates were safely in bed and asleep. Perhaps she was re-enacting, in some strange fashion, what had once been her actual duty in some different situation.

She was in the corridor again, and again closing a door softly behind her. She moved on – painfully and with the aid of her stick, yet purposefully and as if she had a good deal still in front of her. This went on, confusingly and down several corridors, for some time. Honeybath felt that his duty was now clear. He must tackle Miss Wyndowe himself and quietly suggest that she might be better back in bed. With this intention he walked straight towards her. But even as he did so she turned and looked at him. Or, rather, she performed the first of these actions, but not the second. Her eyes were closed as if in the most tranquil sleep.

In the same moment that Honeybath witnessed this startling phenomenon something happened to the moonlight. It must have been a full moon that had been observing these events, but one veiled behind cloud. Now the cloud had dispersed, with the result that a good deal more swam into view. At its further end this corridor was revealed as merging into a thoroughly medieval piece of *décor*: a vaulted roof, lancet windows, and the beginning of what appeared to be a spiral staircase ascending to some chamber or turret above. Before this stood Miss Wyndowe, who had become a sort of Woman in White – or rather some enigmatical figure corresponding to that in an earlier species of Gothic romance. There was something peculiarly unnerving about this small transformation, but it was not this alone that gave Honeybath pause. He supposed that Miss Wyndowe must be in the strictest sense sleep-walking, and he recalled having somewhere heard or read that considerable danger attends the abrupt arousing of a person in such a condition. Grave nervous shock may result. And as Miss Wyndowe was already far from in the best of nervous conditions, on her the effect might be all the more disastrous. So Honeybath hesitated again. And as he did so Miss Wyndowe disappeared.

As Miss Wyndowe disappeared the moonlight disappeared also – much as if the old lady had herself switched it off. A much denser cloud must have turned up. All that Honeybath could do was listen, and this he did. For some moments the tap-tap of the walking-stick was audible, and then it faded away. But in its place there was another sound: a low hum which, although he had heard it only twice before, he at once recognized. Miss Wyndowe's lift was in motion. It was to be presumed that, her unconscious mind having satisfied itself that all was in order at Mullion Castle, she was returning to her own elevated situation, where she would no doubt simply get into bed again. And this meant that Honeybath could do the same – always presuming that he had not already so lost his bearings that he had little hope of finding his own bedroom door. This was an alarming thought, and one apt to conjure up in the imagination all sorts of embarrassing possibilities.

But, after all, was the inference he had just made a secure one? Lifts can go down as well as up, and he was fairly clear that he was now located on the second floor of the castle. Might not Miss Wyndowe be proposing to extend her vigilance to the rather splendid apartments – the 'state apartments', as the guiding ladies no doubt called them – that lay below? What if, having done that, she soared aloft again, went one higher than her own aerie, and began to perambulate those crenulations with which the ennobled descendants of Sir Rufus Windy had been permitted to embellish their residence rather late on in the Tudor age? This was a horrible thought, and eminently Gothic. Honeybath felt that further action was required of him, and he moved hastily and quite blindly down the corridor. As with so many unconsidered actions, this had an unfortunate result. He tripped over some invisible but hard and painful object (it was, in fact, a fire bucket), fell sprawling on the floor with what seemed to him an overpowering effect of racket, and picked himself up amid a blaze of light. Another bedroom door had opened, a switch had been flicked, and in nothing more modest than his pyjamas he was confronting Lady Patience Wyndowe.

Patty was even more lightly clad than he was – not an untoward circumstance in the case of a young woman who, on a warm summer night, has jumped straight out of bed. Honeybath was immediately sensible of the impropriety of the confrontation, and cast round for words with which to excuse himself. To Patty, naturally, no such nonsense occurred.

'Hullo, Mr Honeybath,' she said. 'You haven't got lost, have you?'

'Well, yes – I have in a way.' It struck Honeybath that Patty might have forgotten that he had been put in a bedroom with its own bathroom opening off it, and might be supposing that he had gone wandering off in search of a loo. 'I haven't been sleep-walking, or anything of that sort. But I rather think your Great-aunt has. She paid me an odd kind of visit, and I felt I'd better follow her up. I'm afraid that my tumbling around in that clumsy way must have awakened you.'

'I wasn't asleep. I was thinking about something.' Momentarily, Patty gave the impression of still being a good deal more interested in whatever she had been meditating than in the state of affairs that had interrupted her. 'But where is Camilla now?'

'Well, I heard her lift. So I suppose she must have returned to her own part of the house. Is this habit of hers supposed to be altogether safe? Your mother offered me a kind of warning about it. But I was a little alarmed, all the same.'

'I'm so sorry. But our doctor says there's no real danger: or not on such familiar ground. But Mrs Trumper will be upset. She looks after Camilla up there, you know, and is very vigilant. But the poor soul has to sleep, after all. I'd better go up and see.'

'Perhaps you better had. Shall I come with you, Patty?'

'No, I think not. The arrival of a male might alarm them both. But it's chilly out here. Stay in my room, Mr Honeybath, until I've seen that all is well, and then I'll return you to base. It is a confusing place, Mullion, I'm afraid. You can nip into my bed if you're shivering.'

Honeybath accepted this proposal, at least in part, and not without the disturbing thought that he had involved himself in a situation recalling that of Mr Pickwick and the middle-aged lady in the double-bedded room. The night was much too warm for shivering, and he supposed that Patty had not been able to resist making a little fun of him. They went into her room; she pulled on a dressing-gown, and then departed with the sort of reassuring smile and nod that might be offered to a small boy who has to be left alone for a few minutes on a railway platform. Honeybath took no exception to this further mild mischief. He was coming to form a good opinion of Lady Patience Wyndowe.

There was a comfortable chintz-covered chair, in which he settled down now with as much unconcern as if the room belonged to a daughter of his own. He found himself wondering about fathers and daughters. Did they commonly establish a really confidential relationship? To which parent did a girl commonly first take her troubles, and to which parent a boy? It was something he knew nothing about. You could keep your eyes open for an answer, he supposed, when reading novels – or you could if you believed that novelists have all that to tell in a reliable way about human nature. But he rather doubted whether they had. Did even Cervantes tell you as much about Don Quixote de la Mancha as Velazquez told you, much more economically, about a whole phalanx of Spanish royalty and nobility?

Honeybath sat up in his chair, having realized that this was so muddled a question that it must have drifted into his head only when he was on the brink of falling asleep. It would be very absurd if Patty came back and found that he had dropped off into an elderly gentleman's nap. And it was about Patty that he had really been thinking. For some reason that he couldn't pin down, he was strongly persuaded that she had on her mind a problem more commanding than that constituted by the erratic behaviour of Great-aunt Camilla. Would she take anything of the kind to her father – seeking the wisdom of his riper years? It was this specific question, lurking in his head, that had prompted him to ask himself the conundrum in general terms.

He couldn't recall that he had ever before thus sat in a young woman's bedroom in the small hours, and as he now took his bearings in it he had a feeling that he mustn't in any sense poke around. But he could *look* around, and this he did with the idea of possibly finding out a little more about Patty's character. That she was a perfectly sensible girl was evident from the way she had handled the present situation. He had already decided that she had a clear head, and he wondered whether it contained much in the way of brains as well. The Wyndowes as a family had never much gone in for intellectual pursuits, nor had they made any mark in the public life of the country; in fact it might fairly be said that nobody had ever heard of them. In this they were by no means singular among the English aristocracy. But Patty's mother belonged to a different tradition. There had been plenty of brains there for many generations, at least of the quality that takes people possessed of the springboard of rank and wealth pretty far. Lady Mullion belonged here; she was, at least, a woman of character; and it might not have been quite fairly that she had placed herself among those who feel no need for 'scope'. Lady Patience might be like that.

There were a few pictures on the walls. They had the appearance of having been picked out of the general Wyndowe clutter of such things by the exercise of a good deal of taste, and included a couple of William Ward's engravings after George Morland, a small aquatint probably by Sandby, and a tiny watercolour of a cottage and a tree and a boat which could only be by John Varley. All this told one no more than that Patty had predictably rural tastes, and the same impression was rendered by a row of books on a shelf sufficiently close to Honeybath to be scanned from where he sat. There were juvenile works about small girls and their four-footed friends, grown-up works on botany and gardening, more than a dozen anthologies of English and French poetry, and a number of fat volumes of a self-improving kind, typified by Bertrand Russell's *History of Western Philosophy*. It was Honeybath's overriding impression that Patty had been very correctly educated, although not quite in the way that she deserved. There was nothing else to be particularly remarked in the room, unless it was a diminutive vase on an otherwise bare bedside table in which had been stuck two or three unimpressive sprigs of wallflower. (Honeybath was not in a position to attribute any significance to this.)

The door opened and Patty appeared again. It struck Honeybath as he got to his feet that she had been absent for quite a long time.

'Don't go,' she said. 'Not until we've talked a little. I'll perch on the bed.'

Honeybath sat down again. Patty had spoken in rather a commanding way, and he supposed that she had something serious to say about the mission she had just accomplished.

'Is the old lady safely tucked away?' he asked.

'Oh, yes – safe and sound. But she only got there some time after I did, and Mrs Trumper had woken up and was in a bit of a stew. I calmed her down. Goodness knows how far afield Camilla had been. But she's probably asleep by now.'

'Wasn't she asleep all the time?'

'Either that, I suppose, or in some sort of trance or state of general dottiness. Isn't there something called a fugue, that means bolting after something you want without knowing it, and even having forgotten who you are? I've read about that somewhere, but I don't believe Dr Hinkstone has. He's our GP, and a bit old-fashioned, it seems to me. But he's probably right when he says the main thing is not to badger her.'

'I see.' Honeybath reflected that something of the comfortable Wyndowe vagueness sounded in these remarks.

'Cyprian says that something nasty must have happened to her in the woodshed when she was a kid, and that little Martin Atlay was probably the villain of the piece.'

'Little – ? Oh, you mean the vicar.'

'Yes, of course. He's been a man-and-boy character around these parts since the middle ages. He's even older than he seems – and probably one of our innumerable distant relations, who picked up the family living as a perk. Don't you think the Church of England is an extraordinary institution?'

'I believe I do.' Honeybath was beginning to find this conversation odd. 'Dr Atlay certainly seems interested in your family history. Your father told me to consult him if I ever wanted to find my way around it.'

'You're not likely to do that, I suppose.' Patty had settled back on her pillows as if this were really the start of a sustained chat. 'Did Dr Atlay have a great deal to say when you were sheltering in the church?'

'He was variously informative.'

'Did he blow off about what he called the grand principle of subordination?'

'He certainly did.' Honeybath was surprised. 'Is it an obsession of his?'

'Something like that. What do you think?'

'About just what, Patty?'

'Gentle and simple, and so on. Class and privilege, and different social habits and assumptions and kinds and levels of education. Everything of that sort.' Patty paused for long enough to afford Honeybath a sudden inkling of the nature of her present mystery. 'Do you approve of all that?'

'In a general way, no.' It seemed to Honeybath that here was yet another delicate situation confronting him – unexpectedly, and at what must now be near dawn. He realized, too, that he was being consulted by this young woman, still almost a stranger to him, in a fashion that might readily flatter his vanity. He must not, on this abruptly emerging territory, be led into producing facile or irresponsible remarks. 'But for a start,' he said, 'what are essentially class differences have never for long been successfully ironed out of any civilized society – which doesn't mean it wouldn't be agreeable if they could be. But they do go awfully deep into human nature, Patty. Some primitive people seem at a first glance to have managed, or retained, an egalitarian set-up or ready-made communist Utopia. But scrutiny often shows them to be rigidly hierarchical, after all. Take marriage, for instance. It turns out that you can marry only within, or only outside, a set band of relationships.'

'You mean it would be a terrible thing if I married the vet's son?'

'Come, come, Patty. This is serious, or I suspect it is. And I don't believe that the vet *has* a son – or, if he has, that you've ever set eyes on him.'

'Perfectly true. I was only –'

'Put it this way.' Honeybath paused to choose his words. 'Think of foreign marriages: marrying, say, a Frenchman or a German. It's something that happens rather more frequently in your class than in others – under influences and assumptions that go right back, I suppose, into a feudal age. But if it's wise to think twice about any marriage, then it's wise to think three times about a foreign one. That's because difficulties that seem trivial and unimportant when one falls in love can turn out to be pretty formidable, after all.'

'And the vet's son would require thinking about *four* times?' Henry's elder daughter had fired up as she asked this. 'And perhaps it should be *five* times if – '

'Patty, dear, stop counting. And realize that I've been talking only in the most general way – and saying what any elderly man like me would be likely to say. But on any specific situation that turned up I'd have absolutely no title to say a word.'

'It comes to being on one's own?'

'That's a very hard question, indeed.'

'So you don't know whether Boosie or I ought to consult old Dr Atlay about the vet's son? He's supposed to be our spiritual adviser.'

'I do know that neither of you is remotely likely to do anything of the kind, so I needn't pronounce upon the matter. But I'm grateful to your great-aunt for getting us off to a good start together, Patty. We must talk again. But now you have a second old person to see back to bed.'

'Oh, dear – how boring I've been!' It was unaffectedly and not defensively that Patty said this as she jumped to the floor and led the way from her room. She was undoubtedly, Honeybath thought a very nice child. His eye fell momentarily on the wallflowers as he followed her into the corridor.

12

On the following morning Honeybath accompanied Lord Mullion to the roof of the castle, and then in a rather gingerly fashion along a kind of catwalk between the battlements on one hand and a steeply pitched expanse of lead on the other. The owner of this perilous perch appeared not quite easy in his mind. But whether this was because he was still not reconciled to the flag-hoisting ritual, or was prompted by some other occasion, did not at present appear.

'Octavo ramparts and quarto crenulations,' he said unexpectedly. 'A joke of my brother Sylvanus. He's rather fond of making fun of the old place. And a reading man, who picks up odd things of that kind.'

'Your brother wouldn't have struck me as likely to be bookish. An outdoor type, surely. He gives an impression' – Honeybath paused to find suitable words – 'of uncommon physical vitality.'

'Yes, to be sure. Sylvanus is very much the fox-hunting man, but I'm afraid he doesn't altogether confine himself to foxes and folios.' Lord Mullion chuckled a little half heartedly at this scarcely arcane witticism. 'Ah here we are! The flag spends the night in this locker. There's a Union flag, too, for public junketings, and a Royal Standard just in case the lady comes to tea. Her great-grandfather came and had some pheasants shot for him once – or so we've been told. Just hold on to this cord, Charles, like a good fellow.' With this slight assistance from Honeybath the flag was hoisted, and as it took the breeze was surveyed by Lord Mullion with ill-concealed complacency. 'The battlements turn up on that, too,' he said. 'Fair enough, since they must have cost the devil of a lot of money in their time. "Gules, a Chief Crenelle, Argent". My father made me learn it as a boy. Must mean something, I suppose.'

Honeybath agreed that it must. There was, he thought, something innocently disingenuous in Henry's throw-away attitude to these heraldic mysteries.

'The flag looks very well,' he said. 'And what a magnificent view!'

'Five counties, I believe. But on the east there, it's still our own land that closes the vista.' Lord Mullion's blameless self-satisfaction had increased. 'Boosie says you can get telescopes that work like penny-in-the-slot machines; and that if we had a couple up here we'd net quite a bit extra from the visitors. There's the dower house, by the way, beyond that line of beeches. Pleasant little Georgian affair, and suits Sylvanus and his lot down to the ground. Not that I'd exactly mourn if he was a good deal further off.' Lord Mullion broke off for a moment, as if surprised at having come out with so unbrotherly a remark. But when Honeybath said nothing he went on. 'The fact is, Charles, that Mary and I don't feel he's too good an influence on Cyprian. The home paddock not the right place to sow wild oats, eh?'

Honeybath might have said, 'Nor the home barn, either.' But although forthright candour is the proper thing with a former schoolfellow, it doesn't extend to gossip about his close relations. He mustn't, on the other hand, suggest to Henry that he was reluctant to receive confidences.

'Your boy seems all right to me,' he said. 'You're not seriously worried about him, are you? If he has his fling in rather a pronounced way, you know, it's entirely your own fault.'

'Entirely my fault?' Lord Mullion was dismayed.

'But not in a way you can help, Henry. The mere fact of your being a peer puts him at a degree of risk well beyond – what shall I say? – the vet's son.'

'The vet's son?' Lord Mullion was understandably bewildered. 'I don't know that the vet –'

'That's only a manner of speaking, and you know what I mean. Did you read what the Head Man – the new one, whom I haven't met – was saying the other day? He has to control stiffer sanctions than any other headmaster simply because he has so many arrogant and over-privileged little brutes on his hands. Those weren't exactly his words. But, again, you get the idea. You mustn't expect young Lord Wyndowe to teach Sunday School.'

'As the vet's boy is likely to do?' This idea amused Lord Mullion, and he cheered up a bit. Yet as he and Honeybath walked back across the leads after their welcoming signal to the day's visitors he reassumed a worried look. 'One just doesn't want scandal, does one?' he asked.

'Well, I suppose not.' Honeybath was surprised. Having been at school with Henry Wyndowe, and being fairly well acquainted with sundry similar persons in a general way, didn't – he told himself – prevent his being occasionally quite at sea with the whole class of society they represented. Perhaps he had a vaguely Regency vision of the aristocracy, and saw them as exceptionally endowed to take scandal, family and otherwise, unregardingly and in their stride. Yet here was Henry disposed, it seemed, to lose sleep over what the neighbours would say – this in the most suburban manner. But now there came oddly into Honeybath's head that grimly reticent plaque in Mullion parish church: RUPERT WYNDOWE LORD WYNDOWE. Perhaps the Wyndowes, although they had been (to Boosie's disapproval) Cavaliers and not Roundheads, preserved a strong puritan tradition. Or merely a Victorian one. Anthony Trollope's younger Duke of Omnium, after all, had been singularly prone to distress over misdemeanours in his family.

Here was a point at which Honeybath ought to have let this particular topic lapse. But he was one who possessed a more than average share of curiosity (as artists of all sorts, indeed, are likely to do) and he saw no reason why he should not a little catechize his former fag. 'Henry,' he said, 'suppose I discovered that your grandfather had habitually cheated at cards. And suppose I published the fact in some rubbishy biography or volume of memoirs. Would you be tremendously upset?'

'I don't think I'd come after you with a horsewhip.' Lord Mullion's agreeable capacity for amusement prevailed over any sense of shock he may have felt at this *outré* question. 'But it might be a long time before I next offered you a square meal.'

'But if it was your great-great-grandfather. And if I were a professional historian, and felt the information to be relevant in assessing the character of, say, an eminent statesman – '

'My dear Charles, we've never gone in for eminent statesmen, although I suppose we damned well ought to have. So it all doesn't apply – and you can shut up, old boy. If you ever have to find a new way to the day's bread and cheese, you might get a job as one of those fellows who do probing interviews for the BBC.'

There had been a touch of asperity about this – as well as unexpected evidence of a power of freakish repartee on Lord Mullion's part. But at least he wasn't remotely offended, and the two gentlemen descended into the castle as well pleased with one another as before. Honeybath, however, came to feel that he *had* been probing. It had not, indeed, been about any specific situations or episodes which might have been giving Henry uneasiness over his son and heir – or, for that matter, over his daughters either. But Honeybath did wonder how Henry would have received the information that Lady Patience Wyndowe was giving serious thought to the problem of misalliance as it might bob up within a noble family. He was himself in the dark as to what could have lain behind that peculiar nocturnal colloquy with Patty. But on this – as it happened, and in a peculiar manner – a perfectly clear light was to be shed quite soon.

There was now a good deal of bustle in the castle: more than enough to make Honeybath feel that his own professional business there was unlikely to be advanced that day. He realized that his hosts were not in the position of grandees owning so vast a mansion that they could live spaciously in a quarter of it and run the rest as a museum. The tourists who could pay up and enter the castle (twice weekly, if they cared to) at ten o'clock in the morning were authentically viewing apartments from which the Mullions had scurried five minutes before. It was an extraordinary state of affairs for any quietly disposed family to put up with, and Honeybath could only suppose that the takings at the till were essential to the Mullions if they were to hang on to this place in which they had lived for centuries. No doubt turning the castle into a business concern carried other financial advantages or easements well understood by accountants and solicitors. But Honeybath, who would have found quite intolerable holding on to his small Chelsea studio on any sort of analogous terms, judged it a rum go, all the same.

As he and Lord Mullion returned from their aerial mission they were met by Savine, who was in what was presumably a customary Wednesday and Saturday state of gloom.

'One of the outside men has been asking for you, my lord,' he said glumly. 'I told him it was a most inconvenient time. He said he'd wait and see.'

'The devil he did! Wait and see what?'

'Yourself, my lord. Or that appeared to be the implication.'

'Who is he, Savine?'

'Gore appears to be the name, my lord. One of Mr Pring's men.'

'Then why doesn't he see Pring? And do you mean this young man is still around?'

'Yes, indeed. By "waiting" he meant taking a seat in the servants' hall. It was something of a liberty. But I have your lordship's instructions to maintain good relations with the outdoor staff at all times.'

'Well, well – he's a very decent lad. Send him into my office, Savine, and I'll have a word with him at once. Charles, I'll just go and see what this is about. You'll find Mary somewhere around, doing the flowers. She'll dig you out a lurking-hole for the day.' With this semi-serious remark Lord Mullion departed for whatever it was that he chose to call his office. Savine, having done his duty, departed too. Honeybath himself lingered for some minutes in the great hall of the castle, where a couple of servants were already arranging a long table with various wares to be peddled to the visitors: guidebooks, picture postcards, a range of mysteriously 'home-made' preserves, and bits and pieces of pottery emblazoned with this and that. Having gone in for this sort of effort, the Mullions, very properly, didn't do things by halves.

It has to be observed at this point that Honeybath, although a man of keen observation of what was going on around him, was at present quite without certain of the gentle reader's advantages. So what now came into his head he had to account a very bizarre notion indeed. He had not ceased to think from time to time of Swithin Gore, his rescuer of the previous day. But he thought of him not only as his rescuer but also as the young man whom he had so unjustly aspersed outside the barn later in the afternoon. What he remembered in particular, and still with keen discomfort, was the strength and quality of Swithin's reaction to the inference that he had been misconducting himself amid the hay with some compliant village girl. It was the reaction – Honeybath now told himself – of a youth who is accused of some piece of casual carnality when it so happens that he is rather seriously in love.

This line of thought was sensible enough. But now a wild leap of the imagination befell Honeybath. It was in the direction, needless to say, of Lady Patience Wyndowe. Here was what that strange conversation had really been about. The gardener's boy was in love with Patty, and Patty was not at all sure that she wasn't in love with him.

This, again, only seemed extravagant. It was, as we happen to know, the truth. But now Honeybath's mind went sailing on. Swithin Gore had established himself in his mind as a very forthright and purposeful young man. He might be good at having flowers grow under his fingers, but wouldn't be disposed to let the grass grow under his feet. He had come to an understanding with his employer's daughter. And the interview now taking place he had sought for the purpose of asking his employer for her hand.

Possessed of this astonishing vision, Honeybath felt very rightly appalled. Only a singularly romantic turn of mind would see the likelihood of anything other than misfortune and even disaster in such an entanglement. He had spoken sagely to Patty about unequal marriages, but now felt that he had been far from speaking strongly enough. Such love-affairs happen, and no doubt they sometimes turn out well. But at the start the love involved can only be eye-love and nothing else: a matter of sudden overwhelming physical attraction unsupported by any of those compatibilities and next to instinctive assumptions in the field of manners and conduct and interests which constitute the stabilizing element in marriage. Honeybath, as a sensible man of the world, knew this very well. It was true that his heart spoke to him otherwise. Moreover he was himself commanded, as an artist has to be, by his eye. With the outward eye he had never seen Lady Patience Wyndowe and Swithin Gore together. But with his inward eye he could do so perfectly. And they were as beautiful as Ferdinand and Miranda – or, for that matter, as Florizel and Perdita. You could take your choice.

Having thus let his fancy run away with him, Charles Honeybath was greatly troubled. Henry, he felt sure, would be completely bewildered. Henry, in an easy-going and unreflective way, was the most liberal-minded of men. If Dr Atlay's grand principle of subordination were proposed to him he would merely make fun of it. But this would be because no intimate challenge to the general idea of it had ever come his way. Henry would be confounded. It would be on Mary that there fell the task of sorting things out.

As Honeybath told himself this, Lady Mullion appeared in the hall. She was carrying a mass of white roses.

'That admirable Swithin Gore,' she said, 'has persuaded Pring to let me have all these Mermaids. Of course they keep on coming and coming, but the old man is absurdly jealous of them. Have you seen Patty anywhere, Charles? She must help me with them at once.'

'No, I've been with Henry hoisting the flag.' Honeybath glanced around, and saw that he was now alone with Patty's mother. 'Mary,' he said, 'I've something rather difficult to tell you.'

'Difficult?' Lady Mullion put down the roses, and was serious at once. 'Whatever it is, do say.'

'I really don't know – ' Honeybath, moments too late, had come to his senses. If his conjecture was correct, it was for Henry to break the news to his wife. If he had got the thing wholly wrong, then he would be making a hopeless fool of himself. In this wretched quandary, precipitated by over-impulsive speech, he fumbled about in his mind and found what reflection would have suggested to him as a more than dubious way out. 'It's about the Hilliards,' he said.

'The Hilliards?' Lady Mullion was bewildered. 'Is there anything wrong with them? Are they fakes?'

'No, not exactly that. But something very unaccountable has happened, and last night I hesitated to worry Henry about it. It seemed to me that – well, that there might be some obscure family explanation.'

'I see.' Lady Mullion looked at Honeybath (Honeybath felt) much as if he had made a lucid and intelligent observation. 'But just what has happened?'

'One of the three miniatures – according to Dr Atlay, of an unidentified male member of the Wyndowe family – has been removed, and a reproduction of another miniature substituted.'

'Martin Atlay noticed this?'

'Oddly enough, he didn't. He was discoursing on the things, but not really looking at them. It was only I who noticed what must have happened, and I decided for the moment to say nothing.'

'You may have been very wise.' Lady Mullion had picked up one of the Mermaid roses, and was studying it with apparent care. 'Just what do you make of it all, Charles?'

'The most obvious explanation is that a thief devised a method of making away with one of the miniatures and contriving that the fact should be undetected for some time.'

'You don't think, Charles, that you may have something to do' with it?'

'My dear Mary!'

'I know it sounds silly. But, for a start, this can't have happened long ago. Henry and the children are not much interested in these things, and might notice nothing amiss for quite a long time. And that goes, in a way, for those women who take people round. They declare this or that to be tremendously interesting, but they don't really *look* themselves. But I am rather fond of the Hilliards, and do look at them quite often. All three were certainly undisturbed only a few days ago. And then, you know, you turn up. So it's almost as if somebody had decided, rather hurriedly, that the real miniature must be kept out of your sight, and took a chance that you wouldn't, during your stay, detect that any funny business had taken place.' Lady Mullion paused, and looked searchingly at Honeybath. 'Can you make anything of that?'

'Absolutely not, Mary dear. It seems to me to make no sense at all.'

'I am quite sure that most people would agree with you.' Lady Mullion produced this slightly ambiguous remark with continued gravity. 'The question is, what do we do now? And I'm rather glad you said nothing last night.'

'I'm uneasy about that, actually. But you will understand, Mary, that I saw various rather awkward possibilities.'

'Quite so – and they remain awkward. So for the moment I think you and I will keep this to ourselves.'

'Very well.' Honeybath couldn't help feeling slightly surprised by this decision – excluding, as it appeared to do, even Henry from a knowledge of the affair. 'But there is one thing I ought to point out. If the Hilliards are insured and a claim has eventually to be made, it might be awkward if it transpired that you and I had kept the loss under our hats for any length of time.'

'I have no doubt that is true. Nevertheless, I'd like to think it over for a few days.' For the first time, Lady Mullion hesitated. 'I have to think of Henry,' she then said. 'You mayn't know this, but he has an almost pathological dislike of scandal.'

'As a matter of fact, I've had a glimpse of that.' Honeybath was a good deal perplexed by the final turn this conversation had taken. He had a sense of bewilderments gathering all around him at Mullion Castle. But was it possible that they were, so to speak, only so many facets of a single master bewilderment? He had just arrived at this obscure idea when Lady Mullion looked at her watch.

'Good heavens!' she said. 'There will be a first coachload in fifteen minutes. I simply must find Patty and set her to those Mermaids.'

13

Because she was briskly busy, and perhaps also because she was a little upset, Lady Mullion neglected to suggest to Honeybath anything in the nature of what her husband had facetiously called a lurking-hole. It was improbable that the family really hid themselves in cupboards when the public began to pour in. Their retreat must be to quarters at least reasonably commodious somewhere in the castle. But nothing, as it happened, had been said to Honeybath about this.

He could, of course, with perfect propriety retire to his bedroom (which by this time he was able to locate with confidence). It would already have been scurried through by a housemaid – probably the elderly woman who had brought him tea and pulled up his blinds at eight o'clock. He really did have correspondence to attend to, and the various pieces of professional equipment with which he hoped soon to be getting busy required a certain amount of sorting through. But the morning was fine and already very warm, and he thought it might be pleasant to wander out into the gardens for an hour or so. Two considerations, however, restrained him here. The first was the knowledge that the gardens, too, would soon be full of visitors, or so he supposed, since he had gathered that it was possible to 'do' this particular aspect of spacious living for a lesser fee than was required to view the interior of the castle. He felt no disinclination to thus mingling with the herd. But it did occur to him that if he did so he might be mistaken for Lord Mullion, and in consequence stared at, photographed, and even accosted. This was an idea demonstrably absurd, and he realized that it was the second consideration that really deterred him. This one, looked at fairly, was pretty silly too. In the gardens there might be gardeners, and one of them might be young Swithin Gore. If he encountered Swithin he would have to speak to him. There was no rational reason why he should not do this. Indeed, he knew that he must seek Swithin out quite soon for the honourable purpose of apologizing to him over his own improper suspicion of the previous afternoon. But he felt that Swithin needed a little thinking out first. Why he felt this he didn't know. He was, perhaps, dimly conscious that he had (like the reader) some odd ideas lurking in his head about the young man.

In this exigency he thought of his late perch beneath that fluttering flag. The view from up there had been exceedingly attractive, and it might be pleasant to settle himself before it with a sketch-book until it seemed desirable to find out what happened on visiting days about that soup and bread and cheese.

He put this plan into operation, first providing himself with what materials it required, and presently found himself in a solitude shared only with a few pigeons that had strayed upwards from the manorial dovecot. He decided that they were collar-doves and perhaps nowadays to be regarded as a pest. They were pretty creatures, all the same, and it was a pity that nothing much could be done about them with a pencil on dry paper. So he settled himself down in a reasonably comfortable coign of the masonry and plumped for the church tower as the pivot of an unassuming sketch of the park. It was just visible beyond a grove of oaks. Within a few minutes he was entirely absorbed in initial problems. of perspective – so much that it was with a start of surprise that he presently found himself to be no longer alone. Lord Wyndowe had appeared on the leads, and was now standing behind the artist, apparently studying his work. Honeybath put down his pencil.

'Good morning, Cyprian,' he said. 'Are you taking refuge up here too?'

'Good morning, sir. More or less that.' Cyprian advanced to the battlements and peered over them. 'Bloody buses rolling up, all right,' he said. 'The motor cars are mostly people on their own. The buses –

coaches, they call them – are all fixed up with a firm in London. You have to get on one of the major tourist itineraries, and then you're OK. But there's the hell of a rake-off.'

'I see.' It was a shade reluctantly that Honeybath transferred his attention from the church tower to the heir of the Mullions. Cyprian had not appeared at breakfast – a circumstance consonant with the fact that he was now still wearing pyjamas and a dressing-gown. But this state of the case obtained only for a few moments. Cyprian was carrying a rug, which he now spread out on the sloping roof before stripping himself of both dressing-gown and pyjamas, tossing these garments at random round him, and stretching himself supine beneath the warm sun.

'Business of keeping bronzed and fit,' he said. 'I'm what would have been called a hearty in your time. Just look at my flat tummy. What do you think of it?'

'It seems perfectly in order, Cyprian.'

'Yes – but is it going to last after I've finished up with all that bloody rowing? Or am I booked for a flabby middle age?'

'It depends on what you do with yourself, I suppose.'

'How right you are! Why don't you strip off too? This place is made for sun-bathing. Nothing to goggle at you except those blameless birds.'

Honeybath refrained from falling in with this suggestion. He took no exception to sharing his solitude with a naked young man, and even felt a certain attraction in the idea of transferring his professional attentions from the church tower to a recumbent male nude. But establishing a kind of mini-colony of nudists thus beneath the ancestral Mullion flag made no appeal to him. In addition to which he was not without a certain self-consciousness about his own flabby middle age.

'Do you mean,' he asked, 'that you're beginning to wonder about a career for yourself?'

'Well, about a course of life, you might say. My father says that running this place oughtn't to be a full-time job in itself. Or not any longer, he says. Changing times, and so on.'

'I suppose that when you inherit Mullion you might sell up and emigrate.' Honeybath had resigned himself to conversation – but not too graciously, as the tone of this remark betrayed. 'People in your position sometimes do.'

'My position is very satisfactory in a way.' As if to support this contention, Cyprian stretched himself lazily on his rug, and then turned over upon his satisfactorily flat tummy. 'I like it here,' he said into the rug, 'and I'm damned well not going to be turfed out in a hurry. Having all this, and making one thing and another pay, and owning the power to have chaps toe the line when you feel that way: all that's not too bad, it seems to me. But would one somehow run to seed at it? That's the question.'

'Again, it would be up to you.' Honeybath had realized that this young man was in a sense offering him his confidence and even seeking his advice.

'Yes, I know. But making a career out of waiting to inherit something can be bloody debilitating, if you ask me. And it doesn't much matter whether what you're going to inherit is much or little. Just knowing you'll never go without tomorrow's dinner is demoralizing in itself. Look at my Uncle Sylvanus. You ran into him, didn't you?'

'Yes, I did.' Honeybath recalled that Henry seemed to regard his brother as a potential misleader of youth. It looked as if Cyprian were disposed to see him as an awful warning.

'Just knowing he was all-right-Jack for life mucked up his army career, if you ask me. And now he's merely an idle old rake – however many foxes he chases. And look how I'm being bloody idle myself now. Here's you, Honeybath, pursuing your honourable profession and all that here on this roof. And here's me yattering at you.'

'I'm very interested in what you say, Cyprian. It seems to me that your father probably delegates a good deal of the running of the estate, and that if you took to it vigorously it might be a very full-time job after all. How do you get on with the people involved?'

'Not too well, I suppose. I think they hate me, mostly. Particularly the young men about the place. It's that business of toeing the line, no doubt. And they think I'm after their girls.'

'And are you?'

'Of course.' Cyprian had turned over again, and now sat up with a wicked grin while reaching for his dressing-gown. 'They think it's unfair competition. Not that they don't often have more money in their pockets than I have. It's really all that rot about being a gentleman, isn't it? It can turn a wench's head in the most convenient – or inconvenient – way. One simply hasn't room to help oneself. I think there's something to be said for Boosie's notions of everybody being on a level.'

'I doubt whether you think anything of the kind, Cyprian.' Honeybath found himself not wholly attracted by what he had now been listening to. 'Really and truly, you'd no more give up your position at Mullion than your father would. You'd fight for it, if it came to a pinch.'

'Perfectly true.' Cyprian had now donned his dressing-gown, and the rather artificial bad boy's grin had vanished. 'I'd perform enormities, like all my rotten ancestors. Cut my grandmother's throat in the church.'

'I hardly think a grandmother is likely to enter the equation.'

'I suppose not. I'm sorry I interrupted you when you were busy. It's the idleness syndrome: an urge to impede other people's labours.' Cyprian seemed genuinely to be feeling that he had thoughtlessly trespassed on the patience of his parents' guest. 'I'll see you at lunch-time, sir. I expect you'll have done a marvellous sketch by then.'

Upon this gracious speech Lord Wyndowe departed. He had left pyjama-tops, pyjama-bottoms and rug – Honeybath noticed – just where he had chucked them down.

14

Honeybath continued with his sketch – but now it was without quite managing to concentrate upon it, or at least to treat it seriously. He provided his middle distance with three cows. It was, he seemed to recall, Dr Atlay's Reverend William Gilpin who had favoured this number of cattle in a park as calculated to animate a picturesque composition without irritating it. Honeybath, however, presented his cows according to a classical convention: two facing one way and the third the other, as is proper in a representation of the Three Graces. For their convenience he added a cow-house in the Gothic taste. And then he found himself sketching in his margin, and from memory, the Honourable Sylvanus Wyndowe – who had divested himself of all clothing and was sprawling on a rug. Sylvanus didn't look at all nice. Honeybath turned back to his park and tried to rescue it as a little *capriccio* or *veduta ideata*. But these learned terms failed to make it look at all nice either, and he crumpled up the whole thing and told himself he had wasted a morning.

Was he going to waste no end of mornings trying to paint a portrait of Henry's wife while distracted by a sense that in the current Mullion scene there lurked more than met the eye? He told himself that what was important from his own point of view was his finding the Wyndowes a congenial family. Lady Mullion and her daughters were delightful, and he didn't really find it difficult to like the possibly wayward Cyprian either. Even Sylvanus – who probably wouldn't be much around – was rather likeable although no doubt variously to be disapproved of. As for Great-aunt Camilla, who mingled a dotty existence in the past with a certain sharpness of observation in the present, he judged her to be at least an interesting study, provided she didn't turn up too often in the small hours. But if the Wyndowes were an agreeable crowd it was, of course, all the more disturbing that small unaccountable things were happening in the midst of them.

Honeybath picked up his belongings (and Cyprian's abandoned garments as well) and descended into the castle. He did so in a certain absence of mind, which even extended to his forgetting that it was an open day. No great ill-consequence ought to have succeeded upon this. Since the family made itself scarce on such occasions it was no doubt the convention that their house guests should do so too. But it was clearly no more than a custom to be abrogated at need, and there was no call whatever for anybody positively to scurry or cower. If Honeybath stumbled upon a group of sightseers he could simply glide past them unobtrusively, if necessary with a polite bow. This reassuring thought came to him in the moment that he did in fact hear, round a corner in front of him, the unmistakable tones of a guide holding forth to her flock. And a moment later Honeybath found himself engulfed in this small situation.

It was in a spot he was vaguely aware of as having visited before: a broad stone-flagged corridor which vanished on a gentle curve some way ahead. But the passage, although so far from narrow, was much congested, this particular party being so numerous that it would pretty well have filled the great hall of the castle itself – that being, indeed, the point at which it had been marshalled for its conducted tour. And all these people were in not particularly courteous motion, since their conductress was apparently addressing them at greater length than they desired or – probably – deserved. Honeybath was at once elbowed by two stout women manoeuvring to take photographs (which they had no business to be doing). He made way for them as well as he could, and this had the consequence of drawing him deeper into the mob. Between two rucksacks of the fashionable and formidable sort that tower high above the wearer's head he became aware that he was contemplating a pike of altogether improbable size, and that the pike appeared to be pursuing a perch. So he suddenly realized where he stood. This was the kitchen corridor, and the guide had halted all these gaping people for the purpose of giving them in some detail the history of the domestic offices they were about to visit.

Honeybath had no wish to view the kitchen; it was his simple aim to find his way to that soup and bread and cheese which had presumably emanated from it. But the castle was a confusing place, and he soon saw that he had lost himself and ought to retrace his steps. This was not altogether easy. He had now been edged directly beneath the regard of the guide. She was a grey-haired woman of severe appearance, and pinned on the lapel of her correspondingly severe tweed jacket was a little card reading MISS KINDER-SCOUT. Honeybath found this irrationally alarming. And he had also become aware that several serious American faces were turned his way and that he was being curiously regarded through several pairs of bizarrely shaped American spectacles. This puzzled him. Even if he were a little discomposed he couldn't, surely, have anything actually arresting about his appearance? But in fact – it dawned on him – he had, since he was carrying a travelling rug over which was draped a pair of brilliantly coloured and variegated silk pyjamas. And now one of the stout women was positively positioning herself to photograph him. It was to be presumed that she had identified him as Lord Mullion's valet.

Honeybath decided – foolishly, as it turned out – that he must make a resolute break for freedom. He raised a frankly minatory hand at the camera-woman, turned, and pushed his way out of the crush. Then he hurried back down the corridor. As he did so. and with what could only be called enhanced folly, he nervously bundled up the pyjamas and concealed them within the folds of the rug.

'One moment, please!'

The words came from Miss Kinder-Scout, but to Honeybath's sense might have been uttered by what the poet Shelley describes as the dreaded voice of Demogorgon. He froze in his tracks.

'It will be best,' Miss Kinder-Scout said (in fact quite calmly), 'that we proceed as a party. It is something insisted upon by Lord Mullion's insurers. If anybody wishing to cut short his visit will kindly raise a hand, his convenience can, of course, be met at once.'

Honeybath felt unable to raise a hand – like a child at school who seeks to be 'excused'. He felt even more unable to make his way up to Miss Kinder-Scout and explain himself as Charles Honeybath, RA, temporary limner in ordinary to the Earl of Mullion. He fell meekly into line at the tail of the mob.

It was in this state, already sadly demoralized, that a fresh charge of the unaccountable was, as it were, exploded under his nose. The party had moved on towards the kitchen, but had again been halted for some further explanatory word on the part of the untiring Miss Kinder-Scout. Honeybath found himself looking at the head of a basset-hound in blurry charcoal. He found himself looking at a pile of oily apples and grapes. And hanging between these he found himself looking at two familiar, watercolours. Or rather, they ought to have been familiar, but were not. He had certainly never seen these two little sketches of French river scenes before.

For a moment Honeybath felt that he must have gone quite mad, and was viewing nothing veridically there on the wall but merely a hallucination of his own conjuring up. But he was a man quick to rally in a moment of crisis, and he did so now.

'Miss Kinder-Scout,' he said in a voice sufficiently loud to carry down the corridor, 'I wonder whether you can tell me anything about these two interesting pictures?'

Miss Kinder-Scout, if slightly surprised, was gratified by this meritorious curiosity on the part of her late suspect, and she joined him at once.

'My name is Honeybath,' Honeybath said in a lower tone. 'Lord Mullion – whose guest I happen to be – has told me that you take a particular interest in the pictures, even the unimportant ones. Does anything strike you about those two watercolours by Miss Camilla Wyndowe?'

'Nothing whatever.' Miss Kinder-Scout had adjusted herself to this new situation without difficulty. 'Except that they are not those that hung there quite recently.'

'That hung there last night, as it happens.'

'How very odd! I have occasionally pointed out the two sketches hanging here as being of some interest, as painted by a member of the family. People like to be shown that sort of thing. Perhaps Mullion decided to change the family exhibits.'

'It's extremely improbable, surely, that Henry would do anything of the kind.'

'So it is. Perhaps it was Camilla herself.'

'She does seem a little unpredictable. But it would be a most purposeless vagary, it seems to me.' Honeybath uttered this complete untruth (as it happened to be) unblushingly. He was coming to feel that Mullion Castle was a place, at least at present, where one ought to think twice before expressing one's true mind. 'Don't you think, Miss Kinder-Scout?' he added politely.

'I doubt whether it is my business to think about the matter at all. None of Miss Wyndowe's sketches can be of the slightest commercial value, and one brace of them is as good as another. From the point of view of security – which is my business here – the matter cannot be of the slightest consequence.' Miss Kinder-Scout pronounced this judgement very crisply indeed, but Honeybath was nevertheless not sure that she was expressing her true mind either. 'And now,' she added, 'I must shove this lot through, or the next lot will be breathing down our necks.'

Honeybath felt that he was dismissed. But at least he now had licence to withdraw without being shouted at. The memory of his late humiliation in this regard prompted him to take a slightly tart farewell of this bossy female.

'Perhaps I ought to explain,' he said, 'that I am not concealing some valuable object beneath this confounded rug. What is bundled up inside it is merely Lord Wyndowe's pyjama-suit.'

'Indeed, Mr Honeybath?' Miss Kinder-Scout was not receiving this information well, and it had to be supposed that she thought such a state of affairs could be the consequence only of some unseemly frolic. 'The last thing that Lord Wyndowe mislaid around the castle was a cigarette case. Not that he had mislaid it.'

'Yes,' Honeybath said. 'I heard about that.' And he made the best of his retreat. It involved the hazard of a further entanglement with Lord Mullion's customers, since it was in fact true that another group was following hard upon Miss Kinder-Scout's. The castle, unlike so many modern shops and offices, didn't firmly shut itself up during a luncheon interval. Honeybath was now considerably perturbed. He felt, perhaps needlessly, that the mere possession of Cyprian's rug and cast-off garments rendered him immediately conspicuous and ridiculous. And his situation, or his sense of it, was not improved by the absurd fact that he didn't know what refuge he was making for. The castle was now – to echo a feeble joke of Dr Atlay's – alarmingly Wyndoweless. He hadn't a notion in what direction lay the nooks in which the family and its servants had respectively ensconced themselves. He was in a nightmarish world of polyglot persons being herded through the place by half a dozen females part of whose job was to keep a sharp eye open for anomalous and suspicious characters.

This harassing phase of his experience, however, ended abruptly when he made one further desperate turn and found himself in momentary solitude before the door of the library. He paused to collect himself and take breath. As he did so the library door opened and Dr Atlay stood framed in it. The appearance of a familiar character who was virtually a member of the household ought to have been entirely reassuring. Yet this was by no means the case. The vicar, as if he had caught some instant infection from Honeybath himself, was in a state of marked agitation. He was as pale as a sheet before sheets had formed the bad habit of taking on delicate pastel shades, and he was now staring at Honeybath much as if he had been detected in the commission of some hideous crime.

Here was a more extraordinary circumstance. Honeybath's mind – disposed, as it was, to take flying leaps into conjecture which might be inspired or disastrous as the case proved to be – flew at once to that odd occasion in the library the evening before. He saw again in his mind's eye the little group standing in front of the showcase in which reposed the three Hilliard miniatures – or rather the two authentic Hilliard miniatures and the spurious one. He had judged it curious that Atlay, apparently well-informed on such matters, had failed to observe the fact that one young man had, so to speak, changed himself into quite another young man. Was it not – and the speculation had come to him before – conceivable that Atlay himself had perpetrated the substitution? Was it not equally conceivable that the man had now been all but detected in a repeat performance of the same atrocious perfidy? As he asked himself this shocking question Honeybath's acute visualizing faculty produced that kind of small flashback in slow motion favoured by television cameras when concerning themselves with athletic occasions. The bowler delivers the ball once more, and you decide for yourself whether the umpire has been justified in making that fatal gesture of dismissal from the crease. Atlay, Honeybath now saw, in the very moment of finding himself observed, had hastily thrust something into a pocket in his decorous clerical attire.

But now that wretched man controlled himself. He advanced upon Honeybath and shook hands – much as if the two men were Frenchmen or Germans given to this exercise upon every possible occasion.

'Good morning,' Honeybath said. 'You seem upset.'

'Upset? Not at all. Or, rather, yes indeed.' Having had this surprising second thought, Dr Atlay paused for a moment. 'The news is most upsetting, is it not? Dr Hinkstone has been sent for. He proved, unfortunately, to be out on his rounds. But he is expected any time now. Meanwhile, we must hope for the best.'

'News? I haven't heard any news. Has somebody been taken ill?'

'Ah! Well, it is only an hour ago that Mrs Trumper telephoned down to Lady Mullion. Mrs Trumper felt that Camilla Wyndowe ought not to be left alone. Fortunately she is a qualified nurse, and presumably knows what to do meantime. I suppose that some sort of seizure must be in question.'

'I am very sorry to hear it.' For the moment, Honeybath's suspicions about Dr Atlay went out of his head. 'When did this happen?'

'Presumably in the night, but the details are unknown to me. I heard Patty Wyndowe say something about her great-aunt's having had one of her wandering fits. It may have overtaxed her strength.'

'I see.' Honeybath was distressed to think that more decisive action on his own part might have cut short Miss Wyndowe's injudicious peregrinations. He refrained, however, from taking up this point with the vicar. He believed himself to have a shrewd notion of what Miss Wyndowe had been about, and that the less said about it for the present the better. He also felt rather strongly that it was with Henry that he ought to be trying to resolve such perplexities as beset him. 'You must have known Miss Wyndowe,' he said, 'for many years?'

'Yes, indeed. She is an old lady, now, and it may be that we have to fear the worst.' Dr Atlay advanced this consideration with a kind of routine clerical unction. 'It is hard to tell how her death would affect the matter.'

'I beg your pardon?' Honeybath felt he had been offered a curiously inconsequent remark.

'Various family matters and interests, I mean.' Dr Atlay, who had not really shed his mysterious initial agitation, produced this amplification in some confusion. 'Camilla Wyndowe was the only child of the late Lord Sylvanus Wyndowe, who was himself one of only two children of Henry's grandfather, the twelfth earl. So Camilla may be a woman of some property. One cannot help thinking of these things at such a time, although assuredly one ought not to do so.'

'I suppose not.' Honeybath didn't believe that Dr Atlay had in fact been thinking of this, and his former suspicions returned to him. But was it really rational to imagine that this almost venerable clergyman went round picking up unconsidered trifles in the houses of the nobility and gentry of the neighbourhood? The idea was not unattractive in itself, answering to a strain of mild anticlericalism in Charles Honeybath. Yet when one considered it one had to acknowledge the notion as more painful than absurd – but as pretty absurd too. If Atlay were pursuing some dark design it was of a more arcane sort than pilfering costly trinkets. Having arrived at this not very illuminating conclusion, Honeybath glanced at his watch. 'Dear me!' he said. 'Can you tell me where on earth to find the Mullions? I was late for their luncheon yesterday, and mustn't be remiss in the same way today.'

'Let us go together, my dear Honeybath, and I will venture to propose myself as an addition to their board. It is a privilege I enjoy while working on all those very interesting Wyndowe family papers.'

15

It transpired that the family had in fact fled the castle, as was their custom when an open day coincided with fine weather. Their retreat, however, was only to a small walled garden beyond the moat, upon the sole entrance to which it was possible to turn a key. In this *hortus conclusus*, which was entirely devoted to roses and might have suggested to an instructed taste the setting of some medieval allegorical poem current long before Sir Rufus Windy had made any impact upon history, a simple repast had been laid out on a long table. The company, which was dotted around on garden chairs in a manner only moderately sociable, was more numerous than Honeybath would have expected, the explanation being that Sylvanus Wyndowe, accompanied by his wife and three daughters, had dropped in to share the simple meal.

Honeybath was introduced to the female members of this fresh contingent. Mrs Wyndowe and her girls were built on much the same scale, evinced approximately the same coloration, and talked quite as loudly as Sylvanus himself. It seemed to Honeybath fortunate that the gathering was taking place in open air, since the din in a confined space would have been far from pleasing. Even so, the gathering being scattered as it was and with a good deal of long-distance communication going on, there was a decided effect of decibels flying around. The impression of this was the more striking because all the Wyndowes had at the same time an air of being properly subdued as a consequence of their great-aunt's sudden illness. What they didn't betray was any consciousness of being under observation. Yet this they certainly were, since from the uppermost windows of the castle they were being intermittently stared down upon by the wandering hordes. Honeybath even wondered whether this was an entirely inadvertent state of affairs, or whether the landed classes at their unassuming refection in fact constituted part of the show.

He had the further thought that he was surrounded by a distinctly matriarchal society. Lady Mullion was much more in command of her family than her husband was, and it was a role which it could be felt that Patty would take over at need. If Cyprian, for instance, who liked the idea of making his inferiors toe the line, had to be constrained to toe the line himself, it would be his mother, seconded by the firmness of Patty and the vehemence of Boosie, who would do the job. And the Sylvanus Wyndowes somehow hinted a similar state of affairs. Sylvanus himself might be a satyr abroad, but seemed (even at his loudest) much more subdued in his domestic circle. He seemed, moreover, keener to talk to Cyprian than Cyprian was to talk to him. He had already betrayed to Honeybath a feeling that he lived amid a monstrous regiment of women, and it looked as if in this context 'regiment' was to be taken in the strict sense proposed by John Knox. Honeybath was reflecting on this no doubt sad state of affairs when he found that Boosie Wyndowe, carrying a large plate of sandwiches, had sat down beside him.

'Patty alleges,' Boosie said, 'that you and she held a long confabulation in the small hours. Is that true?'

'Perfectly true.'

'Well, she doesn't waste much time, does she? Can I book in for tonight? I'd like to be told a lot about artists and people of that sort.'

'I'll be a mine of information, Boosie. But it needn't involve our both losing sleep. As you must have gathered, Patty and I got talking because we were both involved in your great-aunt's unfortunate wandering.'

'I can't think why Mrs Trumper doesn't lock up the old dear at night. It would be perfectly simple.'

'I scarcely think so. Miss Wyndowe strikes me as being, at least in some ways, a strong-minded woman.'

'It doesn't prevent her being as mad as a March hare. And she was that, it seems, long before I was born.' Boosie spoke as if this were a very long time ago indeed. 'Everybody is very close about Great-aunt Camilla. Patty and I believe she has a guilty secret. My idea is that she was mixed up in a divorce when divorces weren't thought proper.'

'I think that rather improbable, Boosie. Unmarried ladies really very seldom got themselves mixed up in divorces. At least that's how I remember it.'

'Then she was just in an illicit relationship with somebody. I expect it was Dr Atlay.'

'My dear child!'

'Well, they've always been rather thick, those two. And they must be about the same age. Dr Atlay has put in a lot of time being what you might call solicitous about Great-aunt Camilla. And look how upset he can be seen to be now. That's because of the old duck's sudden illness. I expect they were lovers, don't you? They were reading a religious book together in an arbour, like those people in Dante, and it suddenly came all over them. And it would be awfully serious, of course, in Dr Atlay's case, because of his being a clergyman. Clergymen aren't like us; they're absolutely forbidden fornication and adultery. So that would make Great-aunt Camilla feel particularly bad. She was driven insane by remorse.'

It was impossible to tell whether Lady Lucy Wyndowe was advancing these monstrous conjectures seriously, or whether she supposed herself to be achieving a species of wit habitual among fully grown-up persons. But at least the general proposition that there was something mysterious about Miss Wyndowe's past was persuasive enough. That sensible woman Lady Mullion had admitted to a conviction that it was so. As for Honeybath himself, he had advanced to a theory of it not utterly remote from the field of Boosie's imagination. It certainly hadn't occurred to him, however, to insert Dr Atlay into his picture, and he was wondering whether there could conceivably be any sense in this when the alfresco luncheon party was subjected to a minor interruption. Savine had appeared in the garden; being sombrely attired in the manner appropriate to his

117

calling, and the gentry being for the most part summery and therefore gay in suggestion, the effect was rather like that of the arrival of the ominous messenger Monsieur Mercad, upon the innocent *fête champêtre* at the close of *Love's Labour's Lost*. Savine advanced upon Lady Mullion (who thus became a Princess of France) and murmured discreetly in her ear. Lady Mullion immediately rose and, without word spoken, accompanied him out of the garden. The whole company was silent for a moment. What had happened, everybody knew, was the arrival of Dr Hinkstone at the castle. Even Sylvanus Wyndowe was briefly subdued. But anything of the kind being uncongenial to him for long, he almost at once treated the company to a vociferous shout.

'The old sawbones, eh?' he bellowed with Dickensian vigour. 'Just in the nick, perhaps. Haul the old girl back from the brink by her short hair, if you ask me. Devilish smart at his work, Hinkstone. Always take a fence with more confidence myself when I know he's out with us.'

It had to be presumed from this that the family doctor (although apparently advanced in years) was a keen fox-hunting man. Cyprian seemed to find his uncle's remarks entertaining and it was perhaps because he was going to produce some indecorous response that his father produced an abrupt change of topic, looking round to collect everybody's attention as he did so.

'Interesting thing this morning,' Lord Mullion said. 'That lad Gore came to see me. Offended dear old Savine by showing he felt he had a right to do so. And so he had, of course. He said he wanted to better himself.'

'Was that his expression, papa?' Patty asked.

'Not exactly, perhaps. Rather a well-spoken boy, as a matter of fact. It seems he did more at school than you'd expect in the way of all those certificates they go after. Came into the gardens as one of Pring's assistants just because it seemed the thing to do – his father, Ammon Gore, having been there before him. Wants to go to some sort of college now, it seems, and thought he ought to consult me.'

'And what did you say, papa?'

'I said I'd back him, of course. Laudable ambition, wouldn't you say, Patty? As a matter of fact, I said I'd foot the bill. Gores around here for a long time, you know. He seemed a little taken aback.'

'As he well might.' Patty's tone showed every intention of sounding tart – but it seemed to Honeybath that her colour betrayed her. At least young Swithin hadn't (as Honeybath had suspected on first hearing of the interview) made a formal request for Lady Patience's hand. But Honeybath was far from reassured about the relationship (or non-relationship) of these two young people. He was wondering what more Patty might choose to say when Sylvanus came in on the talk in his customary roaring manner.

'I don't know this pushing boy,' he shouted, 'but I do remember his father – and his grandfather too, for that matter. Name of Abel, I think. Ugly devils, both of them, but decent workers enough.'

'I think you've been splendid, papa.' Boosie came out with this with remarkable warmth, so that Honeybath wondered whether she was in her sister's secret (presuming that Patty, like her great-aunt, *had* a secret). But this forthrightness was at once otherwise explained as being the issue of Boosie's political persuasions, which were at present vehemently egalitarian. In any decent society, she went on to assert, all garden boys would go to college and as a necessary consequence end up as Prime Ministers or (at the least) Fellows of the Royal Society. Lord Mullion, who plainly held the sagacity of both his daughters in high regard, was perfectly willing to agree with this proposition, and it was left to Cyprian to offer a somewhat satirical commentary. He knew Swithin Gore, and was inclined to judge him too big for his boots. Nevertheless, he added, the chap had decent instincts in his way. Only yesterday he'd rescued Cyprian's tennis things from the rain and handed them over in a proper fashion at a back door of the castle.

The party now showed signs of breaking up – chiefly, perhaps, because Sylvanus Wyndowe had finished the wine provided with the meal. It may also have been felt it was time they all displayed a becoming desire to hear Dr Hinkstone's report on their sick relative. But Honeybath rather strongly felt another urgency. It was time he faced up to Henry on a related matter. With this end in view, he managed to detain his old schoolfellow in the convenient seclusion of the rose-garden.

'Henry,' he said firmly, 'you remember my speaking to you about those two watercolours?'

'Watercolours, my dear chap?' It was almost as if Lord Mullion, that most innocent of men, was being disingenuously evasive.

'Yes, watercolours. Something uncommonly odd has happened to them. Those Italian scenes have vanished since we were all looking at them. And two French ones have turned up in their place.'

'Good Lord!'

'I don't want your Good Lords,' Honeybath said – much as if he had summoned young Henry Wyndowe into the prefectorial presence. 'Are you responsible?'

'No, I am not.' Lord Mullion, in his turn, spoke as with the confidence of a privileged if hazardous position: that of the personal serf of his senior, whose word would be believed. 'There would have been no point in it.'

'But somebody might have thought there would be a point in it?'

'Yes. Yes, certainly. We'd better sit down.'

So the two gentlemen sat down, surrounded by roses. Honeybath did so not without at least momentary misgiving; he was perhaps going venturesomely and even impertinently out on a limb.

'Perhaps I ought to have held my tongue,' he said. 'But I pointed the thing out to one of those women: Miss Kinder-Scout.'

'Ah!' Lord Mullion appeared relieved. 'Well, Bella Kinder-Scout is all right. A *good* scout, you might say.' This joke being without much effect, he added, 'I can't, you know, tell you all that.'

'My dear Henry, there's no reason why you should.'

'No, no – I don't mean anything of that kind. I simply don't know myself, you see. And what my father knew, I don't know. He was always on the cagey side on family matters. Hated scandal, and so on. Feel a little that way myself.'

'Of course Camilla did go to Italy?'

'Of course, of course. Plain as pikestaff, eh? Came a bad purler there. Sent her off her rocker at once.'

'Do you mean she was seduced – something of that kind?'

'Couldn't have been anything else, if you ask me. And by some quite impossible chap. I've no idea whom. But – do you know? I've always rather thought of a good-looking young peasant lad in a corner of a vineyard. Sudden overpowering thing, and nothing revolting about it in a down-to-earth way. Yes, I've liked to think of it as something bang-off of that sort. But no future in it. An earl's grand-daughter can't marry a *contadino* – not even if he looks like Phoebus Apollo.'

'But all this is pure speculation?'

'Yes.'

'Henry, you may be romanticizing something quite different. And I don't see why such a misadventure should have sent the woman – the young woman, as she was – clean crazy.'

'Well, she is.' Lord Mullion paused on this inconsequent reply. 'Or if she's still alive she is.'

'I rather think Mary doesn't know this story?'

'No, she doesn't. Seems all wrong. But I think she feels I don't like such buried family matters dug up. It was all buried straight away, you know. And I don't believe my father told anybody but me. So *nobody* else knows. Oh, except perhaps Martin Atlay! You remember that joke of mine about the skeletons in the library. Martin is a great digger of things up.'

'It's fairly clear, isn't it, that Camilla, despite her disordered mind, has retained her grip on the whole thing and been dead determined it will never he brought up? It must have been a shock to her last night when she realized you had two of her Italian sketches hanging in the castle. She probably believed she'd covered her tracks by destroying all she'd ever made. And you see what happened after that. Whether somnambulistically or not, she went to work on the problem in the small hours – in fact rather pointlessly, as you say – and now it looks as if the effort has proved too much for her.'

'Perfectly true. Charles. But at least her secret will be going to the grave with her. Nobody except you and me is ever going to think about those watercolours again. Or you and me and Bella Kinder-Scout. But I can have a word with her. A good soldier. Bella, as I said.'

'Yes, of course.' Honeybath wondered whether this tolerably comfortable view of the matter really represented Henry's true mind, and whether he was as unaware as he appeared to be of anything dubious or unsatisfactory about the vagueness in which Miss Wyndowe's early history was apparently to be left in the interest of family decorum.

And by this time, surely, Mary had passed on to her husband Honeybath's bewildering discovery about the Hilliards. The puzzle about the watercolours had presumably been solved, but that other puzzle remained – as did the lesser puzzle of the recent perturbation of the Reverend Dr Martin Atlay. It was in vain that Honeybath told himself at this point that these matters were (precisely as was the affair of the watercolours, indeed) no business of his. His curiosity had been aroused and was unlikely to let him rest.

16

It proved to be Dr Hinkstone's opinion that his patient might get better, or might get worse, or might remain the same. As this assessment of the situation was (reasonably enough) offered with unflawed confidence it was received by the family as a triumph of diagnostic skill, and everybody settled down to wait on the event. Even Patty, who had expressed herself to Honeybath on their nocturnal occasion as not quite assured that the family doctor was altogether up-to-date, appeared satisfied. And Dr Hinkstone could at least not he judged to be of other than ripe experience in the field of clinical medicine, since he appeared almost as aged as either his patient or his patient's spiritual adviser, Dr Atlay. It was a part of the world, Honeybath thought, in which people decidedly hung on. Perhaps Miss Wyndowe was going to do just that.

As she was pronounced too ill to be moved into hospital and enjoy the full resources of scientific medicine, certain of these resources had to be imported into the castle. A couple of nurses arrived, and were followed by a good deal of equipment in the way of oxygen cylinders and the like, which could be regarded as reassuring if one chose to think that way. Mrs Trumper remained unglimpsed by Honeybath, but her status – or her sense of her status – in face of these changed circumstances gave rise to some anxiety. So did the problem of Mullion Castle as a show place overrun twice a week. It was a relief when the last of Wednesday's visitors were seen safely despatched beneath the portcullis, but at once the problem of Saturday loomed up. Could the castle simply be declared closed?

Telephone calls were made, and difficulties appeared. Whole coach-loads of tourists were booked up in advance; there were contractual obligations to fulfil; matters of courtesy might even be conceived as involved. In such a situation it might remain true that an Englishman's house was his castle, but it didn't look as if an Englishman's castle was very securely his house. Lord Mullion was much worried by all this, and had finally to be persuaded that there would be no indecency in letting Saturday go ahead.

Thursday and Friday passed, with the situation remaining unchanged. Honeybath's professional engagement was treated as being obviously in abeyance, an attitude in which he fully concurred. You can't begin on the portrait of one lady in a household where another lady may presently be passing into a sphere in which no portraits are. Lady Mullion, indeed, had forgotten about the whole thing, and it was only with Patty that Honeybath discussed the matter. And Patty, incidentally, was very little in evidence. Honeybath didn't like to inquire whether she was spending much time in attendance in the sick-room, or whether she had other pressing concerns. He suspected that the latter proposition was true. And this drew his mind – very naturally indeed – in the direction of Swithin Gore. With Swithin he felt that he himself wanted, as it were, to have another go. Being sensitive to the feeling that he was an outsider given to vulgar curiosities, he reminded himself that he still owed this humble young retainer of the Mullions that apology over the unfortunate misapprehension into which he had fallen during the episode at the barn. With this firmly in his head, he took a little walk through the gardens and the park late on the Friday afternoon. It was too late to find Mr Pring's assistant still at work. And when he found himself on the outskirts of the village of Mullion he told himself that he was acting with commendable delicacy in this small obligation. It wouldn't be quite adequate to interrupt Swithin as he hoed and delved and shovelled manure. The proper thing would be to seek out the young man after working hours in his abode, thereby making the occasion a slightly more formal affair.

This sadly disingenuous reasoning set Honeybath inquiring around. Two rustics, tackled in the village street, professed never to have heard of Swithin Gore, but it was plain that the denial proceeded from a conviction that strangers should invariably be thwarted in any investigation into local affairs that they endeavoured to conduct. An old woman who was sitting by her doorstep knitting a stocking (and thus presenting edifying evidence of the continuing existence of an industrious poor) proved more communicative. Young Swithin Gore, being an orphan from his earliest days, poor heart, lodged with old Charlie Dew (not to be confused with the two other Dews, who were no kin to him, although each, as it happened, was a Charlie too) in the cottage next to the old forge. Honeybath found the old forge. The adjoining cottage seemed in fact to be two cottages. Or they were this in a half-hearted way, being structurally confused for a start, and having later developed a liability to tumble into one another. Surveying them, Honeybath felt a certain misgiving and even embarrassment. It was his vague urban impression that the agricultural classes of society were nowadays housed with something more than decency in modern dwellings with all proper conveniences laid on. But the scene before him, he felt, might have been graphically described by the poet Crabbe in one of his gloomier works ('Inebriety', perhaps) towards the close of the eighteenth century. He wondered whether Henry could possibly be the landlord of such a tumbledown place. Perhaps Charlie Dew (this Charlie Dew) held it on one of those odd tenancies about which one read in the novels of Thomas Hardy, and could defy any suggestion of improvement or demolishment for life. Honeybath speculated on what Boosie (who had professed to have flirted with Swithin like mad) would think of it as a fit habitation for a future Prime Minister or Fellow of the Royal Society. But Boosie probably had no notion how or where Swithin lived. Patty certainly had.

At this point Honeybath ought perhaps to have told himself that he was committing an error in tact and ought to retreat. It came to him (for in such situations his mind functioned tolerably well) that Swithin Gore, being an ambitious lad, lived in even more unassuming quarters than his circumstances constrained him to, being concerned to save his pennies in the interest of future plans. He mightn't at all care to be run to earth in them by a virtual stranger from a more prosperous sphere of life. But Honeybath told himself that this was to allow too little to a certain openness and largeness he had sensed in the young man, and moreover represented a false and most bourgeois nicety on his own part. So he chose what he judged to be the less unpromising of the conjoined tenements before him, and knocked on the door.

There was no reply. He knocked again, with the same result. Whereupon – and now there was really no excuse for his behaviour – he pushed open the door and peered into the interior of the cottage. It was distinctly gloomy, and in fact the first report from it came not to his eyes but to his nose. The small room immediately before him was stuffy and smelly. It was stuffy because no window in it had been opened for a long time (nor, probably, could be opened if you tried) and the door was kept constantly shut; it was smelly (it had to be supposed) because of an old man who sat hunched over a dull fire toasting a piece of bacon on a fork. The old man and the bacon might be said to smell about fifty-fifty.

'Good evening,' Honeybath said. 'May I come in?'

'Ur.'

Whether this was intended as a welcoming or as an unwelcoming noise it would have been impossible to say. The old man – presumably the authentic Charlie Dew – was peering round at Honeybath through small red-rimmed eyes. The room was smoky as well as smelly. Mr Dew seemed not to judge Honeybath of much interest, and returned composedly to his operation on the bacon. So Honeybath had to try again. He hesitated between 'Can you tell me if Mr Gore is at home?' and 'Is Swithin around?' Neither sounded at all right, so it was fortunate that Mr Dew – rather unexpectedly – opted for further communication himself.

'Be un looking fer lad?' he asked.

'Yes. I am, Mr Dew. They told me he lived here. My name is Honeybath.'

Mr Dew elevated the toasting bacon in air, and through the vacancy thus created spat into the fire. Honeybath was wondering whether this unpolished behaviour was designed to express strong disapproval of his visit when he realized that Mr Dew was actually pointing to the blackened ceiling of his dwelling.

'Swithin.' he said, 'be up wooden hill.'

This expression, although remarkable in its way, baffled Honeybath only for a moment. He was being told that Swithin was upstairs. He looked at Mr Dew's staircase – which wasn't a staircase as the expression is commonly understood, but wasn't exactly a ladder either. It might have been said to achieve a compromise between these two devices, since it was a fairly solid structure which, however, took off from the middle of the room and simply disappeared through a rectangular gap in the ceiling.

'Then, if I may, I'll go up,' Honeybath said.

'Ur.'

'He hasn't, I suppose, got a visitor?' This alarming thought had come to Honeybath quite out of the blue.

'Urr.'

'I beg your pardon?'

'Urrr.'

Mr Dew had quite ceased to be in a communicative mood. Taking his chance, therefore, of pronounced embarrassment, Honeybath ascended to the attic region above. His head emerged not upon any sort of landing but on what was plainly Swithin's room itself. It was a long narrow room which must have extended over the full length of both cottages; it had three dormer windows and a further window in an end wall; there was in fact an agreeable effect of space. Honeybath registered this, and one or two other things as well, but what chiefly concerned him was the discovery that the room's owner was absent from it. Honeybath was actually standing in the room before confirming this observation – which thereupon disturbed him very much. He hadn't been actually remiss, since one can't knock for admittance on what is simply a hole in a ceiling. But here he was in what was now revealed to him as an impossibly intrusive situation.

He took another glance round, and his sense of this was intensified, since there was a good deal in the room that spoke of Swithin Gore in what might be called an intimate manner. To most people, indeed, the focus of interest here would not have said much. But it spoke to Honeybath at once. On a table by the bedside, displayed in what was perhaps a tooth-mug, were some sprigs of wallflower.

'Wait 'ee there,' Mr Dew suddenly called out from below. 'Swithin I seen un. Be coming down road now.'

Honeybath had no inclination to obey this injunction, and he endeavoured to beat a hasty retreat. But an elderly man unhabituated to the particular exercise has some difficulty in lowering himself backwards through a hole in the floor. The consequence of this was that when Swithin entered Mr Dew's apartment below he was confronted by the lower part of Honeybath's person conducting itself in a manner appropriate to a detected burglar endeavouring to escape from a scene of crime.

'Old un to see un,' Mr Dew said. 'Honeytub, or summat like.'

This lavish interposition was of fortunate effect, since it enabled Swithin at once to apprise the situation.

'I'm sorry I wasn't in,' he said. 'Do go up, sir.'

These words, although uttered perhaps with politeness rather than cordiality, seemed to Honeybath civilized and comforting. He went up; Swithin followed him; Swithin promptly lowered a species of trapdoor over the aperture (which would otherwise have remained extremely dangerous), and an entire privacy was thus secured.

'Mr Gore,' Honeybath said, 'I've come to apologize for a very improper thing I said to you the other day. I said I didn't believe you about something, and I was quite wrong. I hope you will forgive me.'

'Yes, certainly – and thank you.' Swithin, who had listened to Honeybath's speech with gravity but without discomfort or surprise, now removed from one of the room's two chairs a journal seemingly devoted to motorcycles, thereby implying an invitation to his guest to sit down. 'I expect I was a bit upset. It was the old bastard who ought to have been getting the hiding, if you ask me, and not the girl he'd been messing around.' Swithin was plainly without any feeling of impropriety in aspersing in these terms the brother of his employers. 'Of course there are plenty that think of a girl as fair game, and it can't be said that nature intended otherwise. But when it comes to an elderly man with the privileges of gentry in his pocket behaving like a goat or a laughing hyena, I call it a nasty thing.'

'I quite agree with you.' It seemed to Honeybath that he had listened to a speech which – however many certificates Swithin had obtained at school – witnessed to the possession of considerable native endowments in this young man.

'Not that a good word isn't spoken of him by many,' Swithin went on. 'There's good employment at the dower house, and Mr Sylvanus is said to be a fair-minded man, who talks direct at you and is generous as well. He's like his brother in that. Do you know Lord Mullion well, sir?'

'We were at school together. I've come to the castle to paint Lady Mullion's portrait. Portrait-painting is my job.'

'You ought to paint –' Here Swithin checked himself. 'You ought to paint Lady Patience and Lady Lucy as well.'

'So I should – or all three together in what's called a conversation piece.' Honeybath wondered just how near Swithin had come to burning the boats of his secret. 'But there's something of a standstill in the castle at the moment. Miss Camilla Wyndowe has had a sudden severe illness.'

'So I –' Again Swithin had to break off abruptly. Anybody in the village could know by this time about Miss Wyndowe's condition, but he was being cautious, all the same. 'The crazed old lady,' he said, 'used to have me to look after her donkey cart. But she never had much to say to me. I doubt whether she even knew whose grandchild I was.'

'Is that so?' This feeble rhetorical question was all that Honeybath could manage, since there had come upon him the irrational conviction that some moment of astonishing revelation was imminent. By now (and in this like the reader) he had only to glance at Swithin Gore to know that he had been born a Wyndowe – no matter precisely on what wrong side of a blanket. It was true that in

Swithin the family likeness was by no means writ large; he was better looking, for one thing, than any other male Wyndowe that Honeybath knew. But to an informed eye it was absolutely and hauntingly there – as it had been upon the odd occasion of Honeybath's first encountering Mr Pring's assistant.

But if Honeybath expected to receive a revelation Swithin himself afforded not the slightest impression of being about to make one. There had been nothing that could be called in the least degree meaningful about his last remark. He had no particular interest in the crazed old lady. and now he changed the subject in the most unaffected way.

'I'll Just call down to Charlie Dew.' he said, 'and tell him to make us a brew, he doesn't do it badly, and his kettle's always on the hob.'

Honeybath hastened to express his satisfaction at this proposal, since its hospitable nature evidently reflected what Swithin judged proper behaviour in one to whom a handsome apology has just been offered. So Swithin hauled up the trapdoor and gave his instructions – this with a certain air of authority – to the old creature below.

'And bang,' he concluded briefly, as he let the trapdoor down again. 'How do you like my room?' he then asked.

'Very much.' Honeybath had judged this question remarkable in its small way. Swithin wasn't being challenging. He had simply discerned that Honeybath was rather curious to look about him in an inquiring manner, and had devised a means whereby he could do so freely and with perfect civility. So Honeybath got up and strolled around. The motorcycle magazine, he saw, didn't reflect what could he called a major note. Swithin Gore was at least so far distinguished from the unassuming class to which he belonged that to him a hook was a hook and not a popular illustrated journal. The whole Patty business would of course be inconceivable if something of the sort were not true. Swithin's hooks, which were numerous, were in fact much like Patty's own, since they were in the main instructive rather than recreative in character. But his was perhaps the more structured and purposive collection: a fact most strikingly attested by a formidable array of mathematical and scientific text-books. There is much to he said for the pursuit of mathematics in particular by persons of simple breeding and irregular education. Provided you have the right sort of mind, you are on a level here with anybody else. But this sage reflection didn't long detain Honeybath, since he was now much more aware of something else.

Swithin Gore was interested in foreign parts. The low walls of this attic room, when not occupied by windows and improvised book shelves, were covered with pictures of distant places. Some were in elaborate if battered frames; some were simply pinned up without mounts; there were old steel engravings, modern colour prints. photographs, pencil drawings, and watercolour sketches. It looked as if Swithin had formed the habit of picking up such things at small auction sales. Honeybath was about to ask 'Have you travelled much?' when he realized that this would be a foolish question. Swithin was not of a generation that had seen National Service, and he was still too young to have been even briefly in and out of the army. Swithin was simply possessed with a measure of *Wanderlust* which he had been without the means to satisfy.

Confronted by these evidences– which, after all, he had been invited to inspect – Honeybath ventured a remark or two about identifiable scenes and edifices. Swithin, who showed no sign of regarding this particular hobby of his as anything out of the way, produced unremarkable replies, and then Mr Dew banged on the trapdoor and mugs of tea were served. The brew was a little strong for Honeybath's taste, but good of its kind. Honeybath, however, paid not much attention to it. For a surprising revelation had happened, after all. And its implications he resolved to tackle at once.

'I'm interested in this one,' he said, moving towards the wall. 'Do you know anything about it?'

'Nothing at all.' Swithin, too, came up and glanced at one of the watercolours. 'I've wondered whether perhaps it's Bath.'

'Bath?'

'All those massive ruins. It might be what was left long after the Romans had left the place. The Anglo-Saxons could make nothing of it, and thought it might be the ancient work of giants.'

'Is that so?' Honeybath didn't pause on this respectable show of erudition. 'It's the Forum in Rome,' he said.

'Well, I might have thought of that. It's rather nice, isn't it? You can see it's one of the ones done by hand.'

'It is, indeed. And the hand, Swithin, was Miss Camilla Wyndowe's.'

'Then that explains it.' Swithin, bewilderingly, seemed not much impressed or surprised by this information. 'It must have come from Grandmother Pipton, that one.'

'Pipton?' The name rang some vague but recent bell in Honeybath's head.

'My grandmother was Miss Wyndowe's maid at one time,' Swithin said. 'She travelled with her on the continent, I've heard. And I suppose she was given this.' For the first time, Swithin spoke a shade stiffly and shortly. He was a young man for whom Honeybath was coming to have a considerable respect. But he could not be immune from the pressures of society, and he was in love with a girl in whose family his grandmother had been a maid-servant. The thought was not quite comfortable to him.

It wasn't quite comfortable to Honeybath either – and rather the less so because of what he now took to be the plain fact of Swithin's blood-relationship with the Wyndowes. And it was a fact – he was now equally certain – that Swithin himself knew nothing about. Whatever the secret of Swithin's birth might be, Swithin had never been let in on it.

For a moment it was Honeybath's strong impulse to blow this ignorance sky-high there and then. But he saw that this, even if desirable, was not really feasible – if only because the present evidence was too absurdly thin. Swithin Gore must have studied himself in his looking-glass often enough, even if nowadays it was only for the purpose of shaving. If he had never glimpsed what Honeybath had clearly seen there was no good in inviting him to repeat the exercise now. There was of course the much more mysterious fact that Swithin had inherited not merely a Wyndowe nose or chin but certain impalpable endowments as well. This too seemed to Honeybath a plain truth. But most people would regard any notions of this sort as mere superstition, and Swithin himself might well be among them.

But at least Swithin, just because he was completely unaware of any mystery attending his birth, could be questioned a little further without any more present awkwardness than that small one of the menial condition of Grandmother Pipton. So Honeybath ventured on this now.

'And what happened to your grandmother Pipton,' he asked, 'after she had gone travelling with Miss Wyndowe?'

'She came back to Mullion and married my grandfather, Abel Gore. Almost at once, I think. My father, Ammon Gore, was their only child. He didn't live long after my birth. And my mother didn't, either. In fact, I don't remember her.' Swithin paused for a moment on this. 'She was a servant at the castle, too,' he said. 'A housemaid.'

'So that's your family history.' Honeybath said – and tried to convey by his tone that he had no wish to continue what might seem an impertinent inquisition.

'Yes, that's it. The short and simple annals of the poor.' Swithin's own tone had changed, and for the first time hinted something very like dejection. 'It's a medieval set-up, and you can't get away from it. We're in real life – aren't we? – and not in some stupid fairy-tale. The young hero goes out into the world, makes a fortune, and comes back again with everybody applauding like mad. That's not me. I don't want a fortune. There are just some things I want to know about and be effective at, apart from coping with begonias. And one thing I want very much.'

Honeybath got to his feet, prompted by an obscure feeling that the moment hadn't yet quite come for further confidential talk with Swithin Gore.

'I don't much care for begonias myself,' he said. And then, on a sudden impulse, he added, 'But I'm all for good luck with wallflowers, Swithin.'

For a moment Swithin made no reply. He had been startled, but now he gave Honeybath his long straight look.

'It was nice of you to come,' he then said. And he yanked up the trapdoor and offered Honeybath a hand down. It was rather like the business, Honeybath thought, of getting Miss Wyndowe in or out of her lift.

17

Dr Hinkstone, being a medical practitioner of the old school, called on his patient twice a day, sat at the bedside feeling her pulse for five minutes on end, and then put in further time writing out prescriptions rather in the meditative and pausing way of a poet tackling a difficult stanzaic form: the effect of this being an impression that something deeply innovatory in this branch of treatment was in hand. When these rituals had been performed he would proceed to the drawing-room, report his latest conclusions to whatever member of the family was waiting to receive them, and accept a cup of coffee or a glass of sherry according to the hour of the day. On the present occasion Honeybath, having returned to the castle and donned his black tie and its accessories, found him thus closeted with Lady Mullion and Cyprian. Over the sherry there hung a slight air of illicit consumption. The mice, in fact, were at play, the cat being confined to her bedchamber.

Dr Hinkstone had every appearance of being a hale and hearty octogenarian. He carried around with him (at least among the upper classes) a graceful but easy professional manner; and like the vicar he had the air of one content to take his well-merited ease in agreeable society at the close of his day's labours.

'Camilla is holding on famously,' he was saying – and this mode of reference obliged Honeybath to conclude that he had been the aged patient's medical attendant virtually in her childhood. 'With a bit of luck – for there's always luck in the matter, you know, as well as the right nostrums – she'll be thrown neither at this fence nor the next one. She's as tough as I recall her father to have been. And nobody was tougher than Sylvanus.'

'Sylvanus?' Cyprian repeated. 'That must be the antique Sylvanus.'

'The antique Sylvanus if you like, my boy. And why don't you get married, by the way? Nothing builds up a sound constitution in a man more surely than early marriage. Impress that on your son, my dear Lady Mullion.'

'I don't consider Cyprian's constitution much at risk, Dr Hinkstone.' The Countess of Mullion, being no Wyndowe, had seemingly to be formally addressed. 'But there's no doubt much to be said for settling those things early. I certainly hope to see Cyprian's heir.'

'So do I, and to have the circumcising of him, if need be. If a lad holds his fire too long, you know, he may never bring down his bird at all. Things may go wrong with him. Just think of your Great-uncle Rupert, Cyprian.'

'We never think of my Great-uncle Rupert, Doctor. It's not encouraged, and I don't believe my mother knows anything more about him than I do. He's treated as the black sheep of the family – which is unfair, if you ask me. If he hadn't held his fire, as you call it, he'd have picked up a wife and kids before he died, and none of us would be perched in Mullion Castle now. My father would be plain Mr Wyndowe, picking up a living in some office in the city. We ought all to be grateful to whatever disreputable courses Rupert took to. And what were they, anyway? Was he gay, or something like that?'

'Cyprian, dear,' Lady Mullion said.

'Oh, come off it, mama. I'm sure Dr Hinkstone knows, and can come clean about it after all this time, without any rot about violating professional confidence, and all that.'

'That's as may be, Cyprian.' Dr Hinkstone was comfortably amused by the turn the conversation had taken. 'But I scarcely attended your great-uncle, and possess no secrets about him whatever. It's certainly no secret that he was without the sexual inclination you suggest. It was very distinctly otherwise with him.'

'He was more of the current Sylvanus' sort, was he?' As he asked this question Cyprian glanced wickedly at Honeybath. It was clear that he took pleasure in airing these improper curiosities before a stray guest in the castle. But Lady Mullion was now definitely displeased, and Dr Hinkstone responded to a perception of this at once.

'I've really nothing to tell you about him, Cyprian. Try Atlay, if you must be so curious. As I said, Rupert Wyndowe scarcely came my way. He was virtually an expatriate, you know. He spent almost all his adult days abroad. In Italy for the most part, I believe.'

Nobody familiar with the mental constitution of Charles Honeybath will be surprised to learn that at this juncture a splendidly amazing idea came to him. It was less an idea, indeed, than a perception – and a perception that almost instantly gained the status of a conviction. The young Camilla Wyndowe, sketchbook in hand, had not been overthrown (whether literally or otherwise) by a *contadino* disguised as a demigod in a vineyard. She had been seduced by her own first cousin, Rupert Wyndowe, son and heir of the head of their family, the then Earl of Mullion. And since the thus sullied virgin had taken up a permanent residence in Mullion Castle long before the present earl's children were born, it was unsurprising that these children, Cyprian included, had never been told of so scandalous a piece of family history. But what of Lady Mullion? It seemed almost certain to Honeybath that she had not been dissimulating her better knowledge when she had expressed herself as owning no more than a vague sense of some mysterious element in Camilla's history.

And now, instantly, Honeybath found himself wondering about Henry. Henry had described himself as having learnt from his father in a general way what had befallen Camilla in Italy. But did Henry really know at least a little more than that? It was quite possible that he did not. Doing a few rapid sums in his head, Honeybath saw that Henry could have been no more than a schoolboy (and his own fag, in fact) at the time that this deplorable family episode had taken place. It was possible that Henry had some vague suspicion of approximately what had occurred, but had judged it altogether too speculative to communicate to his wife. This would have been perfectly proper in itself. But if such was the state of the case, Henry had been a shade disingenuous in his manner of speaking about Camilla to Honeybath – and not least in that stuff about a peasant lad among the vines.

All this represented impeccable thinking, and Honeybath's imagination might have taken a further judicious flight had not Dr Hinkstone at this point got to his feet and taken his leave. Lady Mullion said 'Cyprian, dear,' and Cyprian (who had remained lounging in a not quite courteous fashion) jumped to his feet for the purpose of escorting the doctor to his car.

'Charles,' Lady Mullion said as soon as the drawing-room door had closed, 'do you see an odd connection between this information about the disreputable Rupert Wyndowe and poor Camilla's fanatical insistence that she never travelled in Italy?'

'Well, yes, Mary. I suppose I do.' Honeybath paused a shade awkwardly on this. 'It deserves thought.'

'And the pictures in the kitchen corridor being changed. Henry has told me about your discovery of that. But I could wish he wasn't so reticent about his family history. One just doesn't know what he knows, or what he guesses, or whether there is anything worth knowing or guessing at all.' Lady Mullion produced these thoughts with a certain impatience which she now further enforced. 'The Wyndowes,' she said, 'can be very tiresome people. I think it comes of never having had anything to do with matters of national and political consequence. Not even during the Civil War. All that did was to land them with a lot of useless cannon-balls and the like.'

'I can see your point of view.'

'But about those guesses, Charles. Is it yours that in Italy Rupert and Camilla Wyndowe formed an undesirable connection?'

'Yes, it is.' Honeybath was perhaps disconcerted that Lady Mullion was proving herself well abreast of his own thought. 'And it must have been uncommonly undesirable if it sent the poor young woman off her head.'

'Do you think they had a child?'

'They might have, I suppose. That's to say, if the connection was – well, in the direction we've been imagining.' Honeybath was conscious that this was an indecorous figure of speech. He had become a little confused before the bright speed of Lady Mullion's conjectures.

'Little people like the Wyndowes are apt to fuss, don't you think, Charles?'

'I really don't know. It wouldn't occur to me, Mary, to think of them as little people.'

'Well, as what the French would think of as a provincial nobility – very anxious about their consequence, and so forth. And one has to admit that an illegitimate child both of whose parents were Wyndowes would be an awkward thing. Any family might be a little bothered by it.'

These remarks, although fascinating as representing the authentic voice of a great Whig aristocracy, were difficult for Honeybath to deal with. So at this point he confined himself to nodding his head in a comprehending manner.

'So one can imagine them all covering up like mad,' Lady Mullion went on. 'It's scarcely conceivable that Henry's father – who was Rupert's brother and to come into the title if Rupert died – didn't know whatever the true and full facts were. But it is just *possibly* conceivable that he knew no more than what he told Henry as a very young man: that Camilla as a girl got into some obscure trouble when abroad.' Lady Mullion paused for a moment. 'And one has to suppose,' she said, 'that Camilla had covering up permanently on the brain. And that she did it once too often a few nights ago. Swapping those pictures like that in the small hours was an astonishing feat for the old creature to bring off. I'm full of admiration for her.'

'She is certainly a most remarkable person.'

'But, Charles, what about that other swap: the bogus Hilliard for the true one? Was that Camilla too?'

'Good Lord!' It seemed to Honeybath that he had almost forgotten about the Hilliards. 'I've mulled over how that can possibly hang on to things. Do you think, Mary, that it does hang on?'

'It's much odder than anything else, Charles. And – do you know? – that makes me think that it must be quite close to the centre of Camilla's history.'

At this point Lord Mullion entered the room. It came to Honeybath as a point of some curiosity that he had been afforded no indication that Lady Mullion had as yet communicated to her husband any intelligence of the untoward happening which she had just suggested as being of a momentous character. And this made Honeybath feel that he had himself been wrong in not at once telling Henry about the unaccountable substitution. He had refrained out of an apprehension that awkward family issues might be involved. But this, he now feared, had been pusillanimous behaviour on his own part. He wondered whether Mary would embark upon the topic now. But Henry prevented anything of the kind by advancing a topic of his own the moment he had closed the door behind him.

'Where's Martin Atlay?' he asked. 'I expected to find him here.'

'You well might, Henry dear.' Lady Mullion spoke with an unusual touch of asperity. 'I sometimes think that Dr Atlay positively lives in our pockets. I seem to see him as often as I see Savine – or my own children for that matter.'

'He came to see Camilla, you know.' Lord Mullion seemed unconscious of the play of any mild friction. 'Very right and proper, his job being what it is. Only it seemed to me that the man was uncommonly upset. Charles, have you noticed anything of the kind about Atlay?'

'Yes, I have.'

'Bothered about Camilla, no doubt. He's always been very thick with her. In a religious way, I mean. You know the kind of thing.'

'Well, yes. But I have a notion that something else may be involved, Henry. Something other than Miss Wyndowe's sudden illness, that is. But possibly connected with her, all the same.' Honeybath wasn't clear why he produced these remarks. That odd perturbation which the vicar had betrayed when encountered at the door of the library had no demonstrable association with Camilla, and it looked as if he had himself now spoken quite at random. He was surprised, therefore, by Lord Mullion's immediate response.

'I believe you must be bang on the mark, Charles. The whole thing is uncommonly odd.'

'Just what whole thing is uncommonly odd, Henry?' There was again a touch of asperity in Lady Mullion's tone.

'Well, Martin turned up, you see, about an hour ago, asking if he could see Camilla at once. I said that Hinkstone was all for quiet, and so on, but it didn't seem to me I could press the point. If the old girl is at death's door – and that's my hunch, whatever Hinkstone may say – it's right and proper that a parson should be holding the handle, so to speak. It's only the papists who insist on it, of course, but even among ourselves it's a very edifying sort of thing. So I took Martin upstairs, and handed him over to Mrs Trumper. Only he kept on making a fuss, and it didn't seem to me to be exactly over Camilla's soul. He seemed to be saying that he'd just discovered something it was essential she should know – before any knowing had passed out of her power, poor lady. I said I'd no idea whether Camilla was in a condition to make sense of anything said to her, or would be much interested in it if she did. Then I came away. But I did expect Martin to look in on us and explain himself before going back to the vicarage. But it seems he must have bolted.'

'It's quite possible,' Honeybath said, 'that what he had to tell Miss Wyndowe was of a highly confidential character; that he felt, Henry, that what he'd hinted to you about it was injudicious; and that he didn't want to risk questioning before he'd thought the matter over.'

'We really are beginning to behave quite absurdly in this house.' Lady Mullion had been pouring her husband a glass of sherry, and she now replaced the stopper in the decanter with the air, on the contrary, of one suddenly determined to let the cork out of the bottle. 'There has been far too much mystery-mongering over Camilla Wyndowe. Here she has been, living out a blameless life in this wholly unremarkable place for I don't know how many decades, and we all go tiptoeing round her as if she were a time bomb.'

'A time bomb, my dear'?' Lord Mullion was evidently much struck by this image. 'I never thought of just that, you know, but I've felt the general idea. Have you noticed, Charles, that Mary has an uncommonly graphic way of putting things? Yes, I have felt that Camilla might blow something up at anytime. Accounts for my not much caring to poke around, I suppose. Take all that about never having been to Italy, for instance. We've had that ever since I can remember. No sense in it at all. Except of course, that she didn't come back precisely as she went. Women are sensitive about such things – and very rightly, too. No sort of decent life without chaste women – and not much secure transmission of property either.'

'Yes, Henry, I am sure that is so.' Lady Mullion was unperturbed by this equating of a virtuous wife with a reliable banker or solicitor. 'But do tell us this. When Dr Hinkstone told us that Rupert Wyndowe spent most of his adult life in Italy, was that entirely news to you?'

'News to me? Of course it was. Rupert Wyndowe must have died when I was a mere youngster. My father never mentioned him.'

'Not even in connection with what he *did* mention: Camilla's having had an unfortunate experience there?'

'Good God, Mary, you can't mean – '

'Charles and I have been discussing the matter. And we agree that Camilla may have been as badly affected as she was simply because her lover was her cousin, and a known libertine as well, so that the entanglement would have been a terrible family scandal. We've even considered that there may have been a child.'

'A child!' Lord Mullion was aghast.

'Which, I suppose, would have had to be abandoned to foster-parents in Italy, or something of the kind. And that would be enough to send any woman mad.'

'I simply don't know where we're getting to!' Lord Mullion, whose bewilderment was without doubt totally unfeigned, looked almost wildly round the drawing-room – perhaps with the dim hope that Savine would call a halt to this disturbing episode by announcing dinner. 'You don't think, do you, that Atlay has such ideas in his head?'

'I think it likely that he has a good deal of solid knowledge in his head. Everything that Camilla could tell him, in fact, during an extremely confidential relationship. Charles, would you agree?'

'I'm rather new to the whole situation, Mary, and don't think my impression can count for much.' Honeybath paused on this, and judged it ignobly evasive. 'But, yes – I suspect that Miss Wyndowe has told Atlay a great deal. But now Atlay has felt that he has something he must tell Miss Wyndowe – and particularly if, as is to be feared, she is near death. The real puzzle is there.'

'Something he has just discovered, you mean?' the harassed Lord Mullion demanded. 'How could he have discovered something about Camilla she didn't know herself?'

'I can't guess, Henry. But you'd better ask him. For Mary is quite right. There has come to be too much mystery blowing about your household.'

'Well, of course, I'm quite intimate with Martin Atlay, as you'll have observed. There's even a family connection of sorts, although I've forgotten what it is. But it would still be dashed impertinent to ask him what private talk he'd been holding with another of his parishioners.'

'Shall I do the asking for you?'

'My dear Charles!' It could be seen that Lord Mullion was far from offended by this suggestion.

'A thoroughly good idea,' Lady Mullion said with decision. 'If Charles simply says, Henry, that you have asked him, as a very old friend, to have a quiet talk about these matters, Dr Atlay is unlikely to object. And some sort of clear-headed discussion may result.'

If there was in this some hint of a doubt about the clarity of Lord Mullion's own mind, it was now given no time to make its mark. For as Lord Wyndowe and his sisters entered at one end of the drawing-room Savine appeared at the other and called them all to dine. It was while they dined, as it happened, that Camilla Wyndowe died.

18

Having conducted a successful whirlwind courtship (achieved, indeed, within the narrow temporal bounds of our narrative) Swithin Gore was the happiest of men. Or he would have been the happiest of men if the stout strain of realism in him had not been keeping steadily in the picture the balancing fact that he was also the very junior assistant of the Earl of Mullion's head gardener. The problem here was one that he felt couldn't just be left to Patty, although Patty appeared to see it that way. And it was far from simplified by that rash appearance he had put in before Lord Mullion, since Lord Mullion's immediate generosity of intent made him feel deceitful and treacherous whenever he thought of it. And now old Miss Wyndowe had died; Lord Mullion's flag had been flown at half-mast on Saturday; it was Monday and the funeral was to be that afternoon.

Swithin wouldn't have supposed that the funeral was any business of his. But a puzzling thing had happened, and although he had decided that secret meetings with his beloved ought to be ruled out until Miss Wyndowe was decently buried (for it is to be observed that Swithin's sense of the punctilios is anxious because uninstructed; although clever he is a very simply bred boy; it is all going to be very difficult in endless small ways) – although Swithin had decided this he had now been obliged to change his mind. And this is why he and Patty were now standing on either side of a rose-bed in the walled garden, with every appearance of consulting together about the last of the summer's blooms.

'Read it again,' Swithin said. He had handed Patty a sheet of writing-paper. Patty did as she was told.

'Yes,' she said. 'Yes, I see.' She didn't, however, look as if she *did* see. On the contrary, she looked puzzled and even a little wary.

'If I died,' Swithin said, 'your brother wouldn't turn out to help carry my coffin, would he?'

'I'm sure he wouldn't.' Patty considered this reply. 'Unless you'd made a will or something, specifically asking him to. He'd think you dotty, but he might prove to be there on the day.'

'This chap's dotty.' Swithin pointed to the letter. 'I don't too much quarrel with the custom. Faithful old friends from the estate, and so forth. It's a myth, but not so foul as a good many that now blow around. Still, I'd have thought it ought to be the older men, who dress like undertakers every Sunday, anyway. I haven't even got the right clothes.'

'You mustn't think about clothes, Swithin. It's absurd.'

'Patty, I won't have you teach me my manners. It wouldn't work. And if one hasn't *got* clothes, one's bloody well *entitled* to think about them.'

Patty handed back the letter. She considered indulging herself in the luxury of a row with Swithin. They'd had one or two already, and they'd ended in a breathless access of fresh happiness. She decided against this distraction for the time being.

'And what does the chap mean,' Swithin demanded, 'by calling me his dear Swithin? "My dear Swithin". I call it rather cheek.'

'You are a member of his spiritual flock, I suppose.'

'I'm nothing of the sort. I think I'm either a theist or a deist. Only I can never remember which is which.'

'Why not be an agnostic?' Patty was enchanted by this book-learning on the part of her lover. 'I'm that.'

'All right. I'll be an agnostic too. But I won't be an atheist. That's intellectually untenable. It makes a positive assertion on no evidence whatever.'

'So it does.' Patty, whose vision of the self-educated would quite recently have been conditioned mainly by memories of E M Forster's

Leonard Bast, felt that she was learning about Swithin all the time. 'But listen, Swithin! Dr Atlay's letter isn't about what you think. In fact, you're jumping to a conclusion that isn't written into it at all. I rather think you know that.'

'Well, yes – I do. But it's completely mysterious and rather worrying. I feel myself getting in a tighter and tighter corner with your lot. And a beastly false position, too.' Swithin scowled, which was something he seldom did. It made him look rather like Cyprian. 'What do you mean – jumping to a conclusion?'

'Read it again. Aloud, this time.'

'Oh, very well.' And Swithin read:

My dear Swithin,

It is very desirable that you should be present at Miss Wyndowe's funeral tomorrow afternoon. If you go up to the castle a few minutes before three o'clock I shall myself be at the main entrance and looking out for you.

After the service and interment there will be a gathering of the family and some others at the castle. It will be a kindness if you can make yourself available for that too.

Yours sincerely,

MARTIN ATLAY

'So there,' Patty said. 'I don't know how you can have read the thing as an order to turn up as a pall-bearer, or whatever it's called.'

'I'm accustomed to read things as orders. They nearly always are. And what's that stuff about my having to be at a gathering?'

'Well, it's certainly not another order – telling you to be on hand to help dish out the funeral baked meats. If it's a mystery, the explanation must turn up quite soon.'

'Patty, are you keeping something from me? Have you told your father about us, and does he want to take a closer look at me?'

'No I haven't – so it isn't that. And I think you had better just do as you are told – or as what it will he a kindness if you can make yourself available to do.' Patty paused. 'It's my guess that you're going to have to accustom yourself to that sort of talk.'

'Patty, for Christ's sake! Just what are you yattering about?'

'I don't really know. But some things have been beginning to come together in my head that I can't decide whether I like or not. I know one thing that I do like – and that's you, just as you are.'

'But, Patty, I'm going to be a very successful man, with my name in *Who's Who*, and my humble origins proudly unconcealed. Aren't you going to like me then?'

'We'll see.'

At this point Swithin jumped across the rose-bed and there was an interlude. After this, however, he stood back and looked with some severity at his beloved.

'It's not altogether satisfactory,' he said. 'Something has come over you – and other people too, I think – that you won't tell. What is it?'

'Well, I've been looking at you rather a lot just lately.'

'Have you, indeed?' Swithin considered this. 'And it makes your head swim?' he added modestly.

'Nothing of the sort. And that nice old painter has been looking at you too.'

'So he has. He hunted me down and goggled at me a few evenings ago.'

'I expect he wants to make a sketch of you, sitting on top of a haystack. In pastel, I think, to do justice to your gorgeous complexion and cornflower eyes and cornfield hair. *He* knows about you and me, all right. And he has taken to conferring with Dr Atlay in the most solemn way. Keep your eye on Dr Atlay, Swithin. He's the man who knows all about my family. And particularly about poor Camilla. He was her confessor, I'd say.'

'It's only papists who have that.'

'It's nothing of the kind, you great ignorant brute.' Having said this, Patty returned briefly into Swithin's arms. 'I don't mean quite technically a confessor,' she then resumed. 'Camilla didn't whisper to him through a little meat-safe thing that she'd been impatient with

Mrs Trumper or stolen one of Boosie's chocolate-creams. But I think he kept her conscience, after a fashion.'

'Good heavens, Patty! Where on earth is all this taking us?'

'Right up to lunch-time, I'd say.' Patty had looked at her watch. 'Just see that you do as you're told this afternoon.'

'Patty, if I'm to be shoved around – '

'Do as you're told, Swithin Gore. Toe the line, as Cyprian is fond of saying. I believe quite a number of people will be having to do that.'

'Listen, Patty! I will not – repeat *not* – marry a kind of walking crossword puzzle. If you can't – '

'No, darling – *no*.' Patty was suddenly resolute as well as troubled. 'I just don't want to muck anything, or get important matters wrong. We've got listening to do. I'll see you in church. There will be quite good listening there, whether we're agnostics or not. But afterwards too.'

And Lady Patience Wyndowe – perhaps vindicating her Christian name – turned and ran from the rose-garden. Swithin (left alone, so it was entirely for his own benefit) scratched his head in an elaborate parody of rustic bewilderment. He smoothed that flowing cornfield of his hair. All in all, he wasn't very pleased. There was coming to him – as was inevitable, since he was very far from dull – a glimmering perception that there had been something very much lacking in respectability about the circumstances of his birth. It was a great shock to him. For beneath everything that he had acquired for himself he had remained an honest working-class boy. He disliked the thought of any blot upon the short and simple annals of the Gores. And if Patty was troubled it was perhaps because, being quite bright too, she was very well aware of this.

19

The portcullis at Mullion Castle has the appearance of having been constructed quite as much for offensive as for defensive purposes. What impends over you as you pass beneath it is a series of lethal-looking downward-pointing spikes; what supports these in air is a mechanism of chains and windlasses alarmingly eroded by rust. Now, as long ago, one may feel, the contraption might be released, whether by accident or design – whereupon half a dozen innocent tourists (as formerly a besieging soldiery) would be instantly impaled, like so many cherries or olives on cocktail-sticks.

It was under this minatory device that Lord Mullion, on returning from the funeral, chose to come abruptly to a halt and address Swithin.

'Gore, I won't pretend I don't know why you are here in this seemingly unaccountable fashion. I gather you believe yourself to have come to an understanding with my elder daughter.'

'Yes, sir.' It seemed to Swithin that he mustn't any longer address Lord Mullion as 'my lord'. 'And Patty believes it too.'

'So I gather from her.' Lord Mullion had to swallow 'Patty' as best he could. 'Did she tell me this at your – dash it all! – instigation?'

'No, sir. Of course I was going to tell you myself. Patty is a very headstrong girl. One of the troubles is going to be if she feels she must run me. When did she tell you about it?'

'She chose for some reason the moment in which we were coming out of the churchyard. I don't understand it. I don't understand a great deal of what is going on.'

'Neither do I, sir. I can't see that my wanting to marry your daughter – which I know you must regard as absolutely monstrous – is any reason for bringing me in here now. I think Patty's at the bottom of it.'

'Nothing of the kind...Swithin.' Lord Mullion had brought out this name with prodigious effort. 'It's the vicar. I don't know what's taken the fellow. He behaves as if he were stage-managing some confounded private theatricals. And I don't like your "monstrous", young man. I don't regard your idea as monstrous at all. It's quite obvious that my daughter is well worth marrying. But of course it's unwise and indeed impossible. Anybody can see that.'

'I'm very sorry that you think so.' It was clear to Swithin that his future father-in-law (as he firmly thought of Lord Mullion) was in a state of considerable mental confusion. 'I suppose you must feel that Patty has taken leave of her senses.'

'Far from it.' Lord Mullion gave Swithin a grimly appraising look. 'I conceive that her senses may have been very active in the matter. And how the devil do you come to talk like a gentleman?'

'I don't.' Swithin was genuinely indignant. 'I've a strong local accent.'

'I wasn't thinking of how you handle your confounded vowels and consonants,' Lord Mullion said rather crossly. He was conscious of not coping with this new family exigency too well. 'Cyprian,' he called out, seeing his son approaching, 'come and look after Swithin Gore, will you. Tea and all that.' And Lord Mullion led the way hastily into the castle.

Cyprian approached cautiously. As with nearly everybody else, there had been building up in him for some time an obscure sense of untoward events to hand. This must have been considerably augmented by Swithin's presence at the funeral and arrival at the castle now. As he came up he subjected Mr Pring's insignificant assistant to what the object of these attentions was by this time becoming resigned to: being gazed at by eyes that were suddenly declaring themselves unsealed.

'Hullo, Swithin,' Cyprian said – doubtfully and experimentally.

'Hullo, Cyprian.'

Lord Wyndowe was taken aback – as he well might be by this sudden unmasking, as he may have conceived it, of the Gore batteries before the very walls of the castle. There was a short pause, while the two young men favoured one another with a cold stare.

'We'll go along to the drawing-room,' Cyprian said abruptly. 'There's to be tea there, and God knows what as well. Perhaps it's the reading of a will, or something. But there isn't a lawyer, and Atlay seems to be in charge. There's something frightful about Camilla Wyndowe, it seems. Or the old dotard Atlay thinks there is. Considering he has just buried her, it seems a bit soon to be parading her as a skeleton.'

'I suppose she may afford some bones to pick.'

Cyprian's eyes widened on Swithin at this prompt repartee – much as if he had expected no more than Mr Charlie Dew's 'Ur' or 'Urr' or even 'Urrr' from so simple a son of the soil. But then, quite unexpectedly, he grinned broadly. And at this Swithin momentarily ceased to look stony, and a certain gleam of recognition passed between the two youths.

'I say,' Cyprian said, 'it was good of you to bring back my tennis things the other day. I meant to thank you, but it went out of my head.'

'Don't mention it. You'd do the same for me, wouldn't you?' Almost as he produced this mild irony, Swithin regretted it. Cyprian had been trying to say something accommodating or gracious, and he'd promptly snubbed him. Swithin told himself he wasn't behaving well. Fate had suddenly pitched him into two totally unpredictable situations. The first was represented by Patty, and stretched immensely far back: several weeks back, in fact. The second was brand new, and consisted in the disconcerting circumstance that he was being regarded as some sort of byblow of the Wyndowes. The word came to him from eighteenth-century novels, which he'd once had a fit of reading in bulk. He didn't like the word, and he didn't like the thing either. And the penny had dropped with Patty, he was sure, and Patty was far from relishing whatever the stupid revelation was.

His proper line was to receive it without fuss and then to maintain firmly that it made no difference to anything. It had been bloody silly suddenly to call Cyprian Cyprian simply because Cyprian had called Swithin Swithin. It was only the sillier in that – he now realized – he had been prompted to it partly because there was turning out to be something potentially attractive about Lord Wyndowe after all. Lord Wyndowe was clever in an obtrusively idle-seeming way, and Swithin, who had gone short of clever companionship all his days, immediately took to that. Lord Wyndowe had at least got hold of what was on the carpet bastardy-wise. The bewildered Lord Mullion didn't seem yet to have caught up with this aspect of things. Or if he had, it was only in the dimmest fashion.

They were now in the drawing-room. When Mr Pring was busy Swithin had sometimes been allowed to carry flowers into it for Lady Mullion, and it was much the grandest apartment he had ever seen. Lady Mullion was there already, and she gave him much the same friendly glance as she would have done had he been seen arriving with a mass of daffodils and tulips. But he wasn't fool enough, he told himself, to believe that she would at all approve of his marrying her daughter. Boosie was there too, and Boosie had recently been rather fond of him. But Boosie was a generous sister, and it was his immediate perception that he had better, at the moment, give her a wide berth, since she would certainly be minded to rush up and kiss him in a demonstrative and politically motivated way. He was relieved when Cyprian shoved him into a chair and he found himself sitting beside the local doctor.

'Good afternoon,' Dr Hinkstone said, and eyed him curiously. 'I feel I hardly know you, Mr Gore.'

'No. I suppose it's because I seem to keep pretty well.' Swithin wasn't sure that this was a very gracious speech. 'I hope you do,' he added.

'As well as my years permit, my dear young man. We did hold a certain acquaintance at one time, I may add. But you are unlikely to remember it.' Dr Hinkstone chuckled softly. 'Except under deep hypnosis, perhaps.'

Swithin was about to say 'I beg your pardon?' but thought better of it. He felt he'd got the idea, and it disconcerted him. So he contented himself with a survey of the other persons present. In addition to the immediate family there was only the vicar and Mr Honeybath and Mr Sylvanus Wyndowe. He had a vague notion that Mr Wyndowe, in addition to a wife, owned something like a dozen daughters. But none of these ladies was of the company. Swithin suddenly felt very out of place indeed. The feeling wasn't even much alleviated when Patty, with perfect composure, came up and handed him an alarmingly fragile looking cup and saucer. He took a nervous gulp from this at once. It wasn't at all old Charlie Dew's kind of brew.

'A party in a parlour, all silent and all damned,' Dr Hinkstone murmured to him perplexingly. 'But not for long. I understand that the vicar proposes to address us. Take my word for it, Gore, that I have got hold of the right expression. Do you often hear him preach?'

'I haven't ever. I don't go to church.' This bald reply was a further indication of Swithin's unease.

'So you haven't heard of the grand principle of subordination?'

'No, I haven't.'

'But there is also the grand principle of legitimacy.'

'Legitimacy?' Swithin echoed defensively.

'Using the term in its broadest sense,' Dr Hinkstone said a shade hastily. 'Nobody must be cheated or excluded, you know, simply on the score of expediency or inconvenience to others. Whether it be a sound doctrine I am not prepared to say. And I shall not myself be taking part in anything that could be called debate. Facts are another matter. I may offer a fact or two, if the need occurs.'

'Well, I could do with a fact or two myself,' Swithin said with a sudden effect of urgency, 'and perhaps you can oblige with them. If you brought me into the world – which is what you appeared to be saying in a roundabout way – you might feel you owe it to me to put me wise if you can. I don't pretend I'm not interested in the Wyndowes. I've a very particular reason for being, as a matter of fact.'

'Lord Mullion confided something of the sort to me, Mr Gore, as we walked back from the church. He is very much upset.'

'*I'm* upset. Cyprian says – I mean Lord Wyndowe says – that this Dr Atlay is going to produce something frightful about Miss Camilla Wyndowe.'

'It probably isn't all that frightful at all. Dr Atlay tends to think along what may be called clerical lines.'

'I don't much care whether it's frightful or not. But I had nothing to do with the old lady except groom her mangy old donkey. So perhaps you'll tell me just why I'm here at all.'

'That, my dear young man, is what I understand our good vicar intends to do. He will tell you that you are mistaken in supposing your connection with the late Miss Wyndowe to have been confined to caring for her quadruped. He will explain to the company – and I am sure that it will be with the greatest lucidity – that Miss Wyndowe was in fact your grandmother.'

20

Charles Honeybath, sipping his tea on a sofa shared with his hostess, was feeling (and with more justification than Swithin) decidedly an intruder upon this mysterious family gathering. It was true that circumstances had gained him several confidences, and had even set him inquiring around. And this had provided him with a certain amount of information of a not widely disseminated sort. For example, his lately projected conversation with Dr Atlay, actually achieved only after Miss Wyndowe's death, had brought him the conviction, if not the positive certainty, that the Vicar of Mullion had long cherished, and masked, something like a romantic devotion to the deceased gentlewoman. It was possible that the grand principle of subordination had as much to do with this as did any vestiges of a long-past amatory attachment.

Dr Atlay, certainly, had been concerned to protect Miss Wyndowe's reputation, which was another way of saying to conceal the truth about her. But this care seemed not to extend to her memory. Or rather (and to be fair to the man) once Miss Wyndowe had departed, and certain fictions with her, it was due to various other people that truths should be revealed. And this was particularly imperative upon Dr Atlay (Honeybath had come dimly to discern) in matters concerning hereditary privileges and ancient rights.

And here Swithin Gore had first edged himself into the picture and then come to command it. And 'picture' was a little more than metaphorical. Dr Atlay, it seemed, had not very long ago become aware that if this gardener's boy had a certain haunting if elusive likeness to several Wyndowes living now, he was by a strange freak of heredity the split image of one commemorated by Nicholas Hilliard some centuries ago. And the arrival of a celebrated portrait-painter had confronted Dr Atlay with a crisis here. Wouldn't such a person, were Swithin to come within his view, spot this extraordinary circumstance at once, and conceivably draw undesirable attention to it? Faced with this possibility, Dr Atlay had acted promptly – taking an illustrated treatise on English miniaturists from his own shelves and performing his deft substitution with considerable skill. When Honeybath departed the particular menace he represented would depart with him, and the authentic Hilliard could be restored to its place. It had not escaped Honeybath, when he had penetrated to the vicar's responsibility for this bizarre action, that the deception might be held to have been in aid of something very like a criminal act. The facts here, however, must depend upon matters still to be revealed. And here Honeybath was as much in the dark as anybody. Except, indeed, that he was clear about this: in the quite immediate past – in fact only some hours before Miss Wyndowe's death – Atlay had discovered something quite new. And his discovery had discomposed him in an extreme degree. It was clearly the reason why, hard upon the funeral, he had felt he must conduct the curious inquest now about to transact itself.

It was when he had recapitulated these matters to his own satisfaction that Honeybath glanced across the drawing-room and wondered why on earth Swithin Gore, sitting beside the family doctor, had turned as pale as a ghost. It might have been expected that this obscure youth, suddenly promoted to a position of mysterious consequence among his betters, would be in at least an incipiently euphoric state of mind. There must, to put it crudely, be something in this for him. And as he was already indulging himself in the hope of a wildly unsuitable niche within his employer's family, he ought surely to be feeling that something like a providential leg-up had suddenly presented itself in this enterprise.

But such a line of thought, Honeybath had to acknowledge to himself at once, did injustice to Swithin Gore. The young man was very much concerned to stand on his own feet. That he could now in any sense be thought of as coming at the Wyndowes with menaces would be a notion very far from grateful to him. He wasn't feather-headed, but he did own the self-confidence of his years, and probably underestimated his own disastrous ineligibility as a suitor for the hand of Lord Mullion's daughter. Or it might be said that he was confident of Patty herself, and judged this to be enough. Honeybath wasn't entirely disposed to be judged that he was wrong.

Dr Atlay had cleared his throat. It was in what Honeybath felt to be an uncharacteristically hesitant way. Dr Atlay, in fact, had envisaged some such scene as this – and perhaps over a considerable period of time. But now he was conscious that it couldn't be played in quite the fashion he had anticipated; that he was committed to bat, in fact, on a distinctly sticky wicket. Honeybath had just arrived at this thought when Sylvanus Wyndowe took advantage of the moment's silence to address himself to Lady Mullion, on whose other hand he sat. He did so in what he probably believed to be a confidential murmur, but which turned out to be his customary roar or bellow.

'Mary, who the devil is that young fellow over there beside old Hinkstone? Haven't I seen him trundling muck around the place?'

'His name is Swithin Gore, Sylvanus. I think I heard you say the other day that you knew the family.'

'The deuce it is! He doesn't look like a Gore to me. Ugly clod-hoppers, all of them. And I like the cut of that young man.'

'No doubt, Sylvanus.' Lady Mullion was facing up to this embarrassing moment well. 'But Dr Atlay has something to say to us. So please be quiet and listen to him.'

Sylvanus Wyndowe would probably not have claimed to he a particularly tactful man. Even so, having become aware of an unknown young man now ensconced within the Wyndowe family circle, he might have been expected to refrain from immediately and loudly associating him with a harrow. Swithin's own discomposure did not appear to have been increased. Dr Atlay, however, was glancing at Sylvanus with disfavour and even horror, as if any

reflection upon young Mr Gore and his dunghill pursuits evinced the most unspeakable impropriety. And now Mr Atlay spoke.

'Mullion,' he said augustly, 'have I your permission to begin?'

'Yes, Martin, by all means. If you want to, that's to say.' Lord Mullion's intellectual faculties seemed to be increasingly in abeyance. 'We are always delighted to hear you talk. Dashed good sermon only a couple of Sundays ago, if I may say so.'

'By Jove, yes! You gave it to them hot and strong, sir.' Cyprian, as he produced this untimely mockery, glanced around for any approval he could pick up.

'Cyprian, dear,' Lady Mullion said.

'Sorry, mama.' Cyprian looked decently abashed. 'Drive on, sir.'

'Camilla's death,' Dr Atlay began, 'is, it need hardly be said, a sorrow to us all. And on me it imposes a duty which I am loath to fulfil. To Camilla herself, however, I long ago gave a promise that it would be so. Everything that I have to tell you came to me, fully and freely, from her; and on the understanding that it would be transmitted to her kinsfolk in due season. Or *nearly* everything.' Here Dr Atlay paused weightily. 'One circumstance, and that a transforming one, has come to me only recently, and from a different source. What dear Camilla would have thought of it, how she would have judged it to affect the propriety of what was determined and acted upon many years ago, I scarcely dare to conjecture.'

This exordium, being sufficiently portentous, may be said to have held the vicar's auditory spellbound at once. The most gripping sermon that Lord Mullion and his heir had ever heard from him could scarcely have been of greater effect.

'Camilla,' Dr Atlay pursued, 'when a young woman – indeed, a very young woman – travelled somewhat adventuresomely abroad. This, as we all know, was because she was given to artistic pursuits. She was accompanied – and here was a most regrettable circumstance – only by her personal maid, herself quite a young person, of the name of Pipton. On the continent, and all unknown to her people at home, she formed an attachment to her cousin, Rupert Wyndowe, at that time the heir to the earldom. Nobody knew or heard about

Rupert; he lived much on the continent; he was a man, I am sorry to say, of loose morals.'

'Good God!' Lord Mullion interrupted. 'Then Mary and Charles were right. Rupert it was! I knew there was something pretty specific, you see. But I always felt I'd better make a secret of it. Go on, my dear Martin.'

'Most reluctantly, Mullion, I will go on. Rupert's seduction of his young kinswoman – for it came to that – was accomplished only with the aid of a most atrocious subterfuge – one such as is happily confined, for the most part, within the covers of cheap romances. It was with tears in her eyes that Camilla told me the story. Rupert, she said, arranged for, and carried through, a clandestine marriage with her, explaining that various matters of inheritance and the like within the family made it inexpedient that the bond should be made public at that immediate time. Being an artless, as well as an ardent, girl, she agreed to this. Very shortly after this, she became pregnant. And at that point Rupert revealed himself in his true colours. Tired of his amour, he told her that he was in fact already a married man, that their own marriage ceremony had therefore been invalid and worthless, and that he was clearing out. That, Camilla said, was his crude expression. And clear out he did. Camilla never heard from him again during the remaining eight or ten years of his life.'

'Great heavens, Martin!' The Earl of Mullion was aghast. 'How did you react to all this?'

'I was, of course, deeply affected, my dear Mullion – very deeply affected, indeed. But the strangest part of the story that Camilla so movingly confided to me has yet to come. A son was born to her, almost immediately before it was designed that she should return to England. This unhappy and illegitimate infant might well have been left in Italy. But Camilla, with the help, Mullion, of your father, who alone knew the truth, in fact brought her child back to England and Mullion. It was represented as being Pipton's child, and irregularly conceived here in the village to which Pipton had been briefly returned from abroad on the death of a parent. The father was declared to be one Abel Gore, and Abel Gore was persuaded to marry Pipton at once.'

'Surely,' Lady Mullion asked quietly, 'something of this would have come down in my husband's family?'

'So one would have supposed. But it was not so. The late earl, your husband's brother, was himself a somewhat secretive man.' Atlay made his weightiest pause yet. 'And it is thus that we come to the young man we are so happy to have with us today: happy, I hope, because it was Camilla's wish that it should eventually be so. Swithin is the son of one Ammon Gore, Abel's only child. And he is thus the grandson of Rupert and Camilla Wyndowe.'

For some moments there was an absolute silence. At the far end of the room Dr Hinkstone stirred uneasily, but Swithin sat like a stone.

'And that's the whole thing?' Sylvanus Wyndowe suddenly shouted.

'So I have for long supposed.' Dr Atlay paused – but this time plainly without any notion of rhetorical effect. 'I hope it will be understood,' he then went on, 'that I was not in a position to break the late Miss Wyndowe's confidence, which had been reposed in me, indeed, virtually in my sacerdotal character. I did feel it my duty to inquire most carefully into her story. It is clear that as a young girl in Rome she could have been imposed upon very readily, whether in one way or another. I found myself very much doubting whether Rupert Wyndowe had ever gone through a valid marriage with anybody. In his position, it would not have been an easy thing to conceal. He might well, it seemed to me, have staged an entirely spurious ceremony with Camilla – and later, instead of confessing this to her, have told her that their marriage was worthless because bigamous. But now I come to my final discovery. And I fear I have to warn you that it is utterly confounding. Only a few days ago, among the innumerable family papers that have silted up here in the castle, I came upon a small bundle of letters written by Rupert Wyndowe. They had been addressed to a female correspondent, and must be described as composed in a coarse and boastful vein. The lady, it seems, must have grown disgusted with him and returned his correspondence – which he then did not trouble to destroy. In one of the letters he tells the story of the affair with his cousin. Being determined to desert her, he simply invented the assertion that their marriage had been bigamous. It had been nothing of the kind.'

'*It had been nothing of the kind?*' It was Lord Mullion who repeated this, and the action seemed suddenly to clear his mind. 'Damn it, Martin, a marriage can't be bigamous if it hasn't been a marriage at all, but only a filthy charade! Surely – '

'Precisely so, Mullion. Rupert had to think up the lie about bigamy to get rid of Camilla while keeping her quiet. The marriage ceremony he had gone through with her in his period of first infatuation had been as valid as you please. At the moment, of course, we have only the evidence of a boastful and disagreeable letter. But I fear I am fairly sure that research will prove it to be true.'

'May I ask a question or two, please?' Swithin had jumped to his feet, and it was immediately evident that he was furiously angry. But the effect was to lend him even more than his usual command of confident speech. 'Are we to understand that the lady we called Miss Camilla Wyndowe in fact bore a legitimate son to her husband and cousin Rupert, the heir to the earldom?'

'That is certainly so,' Dr Atlay said, 'unless we are very far astray indeed.'

'And this child became known as Ammon Gore because fathered on a certain Abel Gore, and his wife whom I think of as my grandmother Pipton?'

'Yes.'

'And Ammon Gore married, and I am his only child?'

'Yes.'

At this point it is to be regretted that Swithin (lately Gore) a little lost his temper and even his head. His next remarks came as a shout the effect of which was oddly akin to some of those achieved by Mr Sylvanus Wyndowe himself.

'Are you trying to make a bloody earl of me?' Swithin shouted. 'I'll have nothing to do with it. It's a damned disgrace. It's a load of old rubbish.' He swallowed violently. 'Not earldoms and so forth,' he added rather desperately. 'I don't care about them any way on. But all this. And raking things up. And, as I say, making a monkey of me.' With this decline into inelegant speech Swithin sat down, as if his bolt were momentarily shot. And it was now Cyprian who stood up.

'I do think there's something to be said for getting things a little clearer,' he said. 'If Swithin wants to be Lord Wyndowe instead of me, I don't mind a bit.' Cyprian halted on this, perhaps astonished to find that it was almost true. 'But it would be rather steep if he wanted to turf out my father and become Lord Mullion at once.'

'Oh, shut *up*!' Swithin had jumped to his feet again and was advancing belligerently upon his so recently acquired kinsman. Cyprian, to Lady Mullion's evident discomposure, was equally disposed to turn her drawing-room into a boxing ring. The two young men squared up to one another, furiously glaring. Then – and with absolute simultaneity – they both burst out laughing.

'Rubbish!' Swithin shouted. 'Utter rubbish!'

'Rubbish!' Cyprian echoed – mysteriously but with complete conviction.

'Rubbish, indeed.'

Dr Hinkstone had spoken for the first time – and so quietly that everybody turned and stared at him. What they saw was an old man in a most evident state of enjoyment.

'Complete nonsense,' Dr Hinkstone said, 'and simply for want of a few facts. Our well-informed vicar is a little lacking in information, I am glad to say. Or I *think* I am glad to say. Nothing dramatic is going to happen to the Earldom of Mullion. And Swithin is not the late Miss Wyndowe's grandson.'

'What do you mean?' Swithin demanded, suddenly (and in both senses) turning round. 'Didn't you tell me I was?'

'No, my dear young man, I did not. I told you that Dr Atlay was going to tell you so. You are not Camilla Wyndowe's grandson. Nor are you Rupert Wyndowe's grandson either.'

'Swithin's not a Wyndowe at all?' The question, expressed in terms of comical-dismay, came from Cyprian.

'Ah!' Dr Hinkstone said. 'That I did *not* say.'

21

'Martin Atlay's narrative,' Dr Hinkstone pursued, 'I am perfectly willing to accept apart from one small particular. And his feelings about it all do him credit, no doubt.'

'My feelings,' Dr Atlay said with dignity, 'are extremely painful: a fact I have been unable to suppress. The claims of truth are paramount, nevertheless.'

'I quite agree, provided one has enough of the truth to flourish around.' Dr Hinkstone glanced rather wickedly round his auditory, so that a sensitive observer might have felt him to he extracting more amusement from the situation than its awkward nature warranted. 'And enough of the truth means *all* the truth – about Wyndowes, Gores, and everybody else. But, of course, what one wants are the *relevant* truths. Rupert and Camilla Wyndowe were legally husband and wife. Rupert and Camilla Wyndowe were not legally husband and wife. One of these statements is true, and the other false. I am myself quite uninterested in which is which, since the point is of no practical concern to anybody now living. Let us agree, however, that the marriage *was* legally valid. As I have indicated, I am perfectly willing to concede the point.

'Let us now consider what follows. Rupert, at that time Lord Wyndowe and heir to the earldom, has himself acquired an heir. But being a man utterly devoid of principle, and unwilling to acknowledge his marriage, he is content that this child should grow up on the family estate under the name of Abel Gore. This boy does so grow up, marries, and has a son called Ammon Gore. So far, and granting our first hypothesis, we are on what may almost be called firm ground. Whether these two gentlemen were by right successive Earls Of Mullion it might, I imagine, take many legal luminaries to determine – if not, indeed, the entire House of Peers into the bargain. But as both these rustic gentlemen are now dead, I think I am right in saying that nothing of all this would affect the present position of Lord Mullion. He would undoubtedly be confirmed in it, as would his son, were the question to be raised in any way.'

'Nothing of the kind!' Cyprian had jumped to his feet, and was again in a condition of considerable excitement. 'It's perfectly plain that Swithin – '

'Ah! I come to Swithin now.' As he said this, Dr Hinkstone nodded benignly to the late heir of the Gores. 'And the more readily, I may say, because he appears to be a perfectly sensible young man. With Swithin, moreover, I come to that single small particular in what may be termed Atlay's case that I am unable to accept. I have a little authority here, as I brought Swithin into the world. I fear, my dear Atlay, that you are not very likely to see him out of it.' Hinkstone paused on this stroke of wit, in which he seemed to find considerable satisfaction. 'I repeat that I brought Swithin into the world – and, naturally, as being Ammon Gore's son. But this was a deception. It was a deception, no doubt, of a most painful kind, so that when I became aware of the truth I felt it to be far from my business to publicize it. It would, indeed, have been contrary to the ethics of my profession to do so. However, here is the fact now. Swithin is not Ammon Gore's son.'

'How the devil can you know that, Hinkstone?' It was Lord Mullion who asked this question – and then promptly answered it himself. 'Something not quite delicate, eh?'

'You may express it that way, if you please, my dear Mullion. What happened was this. Ammon Gore, whom I had never attended before, fell seriously ill, and in fact died not very long afterwards in the cottage hospital. It was not before I had discovered that he was congenitally incapable of fatherhood. For what the point is worth, this was confirmed by two of my colleagues, and is a matter of verifiable record at need.' Dr Hinkstone paused briefly. 'So if you accept my word on all this,' he concluded, 'the entire matter can be dismissed from our minds.'

For some moments nobody had anything to say. And nobody seemed very pleased – least of all the suddenly unfathered Swithin. Then Lady Patience Wyndowe stood up, crossed the room, sat down beside her lover, and spoke for the first time.

'I don't think so, Dr Hinkstone,' she said.

'My dear child, there is no purpose – '

'Didn't you say, or at least imply, that you were *not* asserting that Swithin is not a Wyndowe?'

'If I did, it was inadvertent – or, rather, a mere pedantry. Anybody may be anybody, theoretically speaking.'

'Damn it, Hinkstone, that won't do. It won't do at all.' Lord Mullion, as he made this all too obvious point, was suddenly surprisingly formidable. 'Swithin, my dear lad, I hope you agree with me.'

'Yes, sir, I do.' Swithin, after half an hour of mingled embarrassment and acute suffering, looked thoroughly formidable too.

'We're not going to leave this on a note of bloody innuendo,' Cyprian said – violently, yet cogently enough. 'You'll damn well say what you know, you old – '

'Cyprian, dear,' Lady Mullion said.

'You old fool,' Cyprian concluded composedly and on a milder note.

All this was extremely awkward and improper, and in face of it Dr Hinkstone was obliged to change his tone.

'If I have mishandled this,' he said, 'I apologize. Perhaps it is now unavoidable that more should be said. But it must be with due warning, Lord Mullion. For what remains is something that Atlay would be abundantly justified in calling extremely painful. But I acknowledge that one further fact is due to this young man.'

'If Swithin is a gentleman's son,' Atlay said augustly, 'he is certainly entitled to know the fact.'

At this Swithin made to speak. It is only too probable that he was going to say (or shout) 'To hell with gentlemen's sons!' Patty's hand on his knee, however, restrained him for a moment.

'Very well,' Hinkstone said. 'Eventually the unhappy woman –'

'Don't call my mother the unhappy woman,' Swithin said – but tolerably calmly. 'Just get on.'

'Eventually she confided to me her child's true parentage. The boy christened as Swithin Gore was in fact Mr Sylvanus Wyndowe's son.'

'*By God, I've got a son!*' Sylvanus Wyndowe had leapt to his feet, and his complexion was like a beacon suddenly ignited to announce some portentous event. 'Damn it!' he roared, 'it was that little Amy. It all comes back to me. She was married to a Gore. I've got a son, as well as that gaggle of women. Hurrah, hurrah, hurrah!' With these astonishing words, Sylvanus ran across the room, hauled the dumbfounded Swithin to his feet, embraced him, and showed every sign of proposing to waltz him round the resplendent scene of this bizarre conference.

It was at this moment that Savine entered, followed by a parlour-maid. His intention was no doubt to remove the tea-things. He gave one glance at the situation, however, and abruptly withdrew, shooing the young woman before him like a straying hen.

'I'll take him into my house!' Sylvanus roared. 'I'll make a man of him. I'll teach him to sit a horse –'

'I can sit a horse!' Swithin shouted indignantly. Father and son glared at one another, each in a high state of emotional confusion.

Not unnaturally, this response to so untoward a sequence of events became general for a time. It was Charles Honeybath RA who eventually a little relieved the tension. He had been silent throughout the protracted *éclaircissement*, but now felt that something fell to be said.

'My dear Mr Wyndowe,' he said, 'it is fortunate that making a man of Swithin is unlikely to take you long. For it is improbable that Lady Patience will part from him for more than a month or two.'

'And I am certainly not parting with him now,' Patty said, rising composedly to her feet. 'Swithin and I are going out to dine together.'

And Patty, for once in a way indubitably running her lover, took Swithin by the hand, led him up to her mother, presided over a kiss, and left the drawing-room on his arm.

Lady Mullion rang a hell, thereby summoning Savine to restore normal life to Mullion Castle. And then Honeybath turned to her.

'Mary,' he said, 'that young man is very much to be congratulated. And now you and I must get down to thinking about our portrait.'

MICHAEL INNES

APPLEBY AT ALLINGTON

Sir John Appleby dines one evening at Allington Park, the Georgian home of his acquaintance, Owain Allington, who is new to the area. His curiosity is aroused when Allington mentions his nephew and heir to the estate, Martin Allington, whose name Appleby recognises. The evening comes to an end but, just as Appleby is leaving, they find a dead man – electrocuted in the *son et lumière* box that had been installed in the grounds.

APPLEBY ON ARARAT

Inspector Appleby is stranded on a very strange island, with a rather odd bunch of people – too many men, too few women (and one of them too attractive) cause a deal of trouble. But that is nothing compared to later developments, including the body afloat in the water and the attack by local inhabitants.

'Every sentence he writes has flavour, every incident flamboyance'
– *Times Literary Supplement*

MICHAEL INNES

THE DAFFODIL AFFAIR

Inspector Appleby's aunt is most distressed when her horse, Daffodil – a somewhat half-witted animal with exceptional numerical skills – goes missing from her stable in Harrogate. Meanwhile, Hudspith is hot on the trail of Lucy Rideout, an enigmatic young girl who has been whisked away to an unknown isle by a mysterious gentleman. And when a house in Bloomsbury, supposedly haunted, also goes missing, the baffled policemen search for a connection. As Appleby and Hudspith trace Daffodil and Lucy, the fragments begin to come together and an extravagant project is uncovered, leading them to a South American jungle.

'Yet another surprising firework display of wit and erudition and ingenious invention'
– *Guardian*

DEATH AT THE PRESIDENT'S LODGING

Inspector Appleby is called to St Anthony's College, where the President has been murdered in his Lodging. Scandal abounds when it becomes clear that the only people with any motive to murder him are the only people who had the opportunity – because the President's Lodging opens off Orchard Ground, which is locked at night, and only the Fellows of the College have keys…

'It is quite the most accomplished first crime novel that I have read…all first-rate entertainment'
– Cecil Day Lewis, *Daily Telegraph*

MICHAEL INNES

HAMLET, REVENGE!

At Seamnum Court, seat of the Duke of Horton, The Lord Chancellor of England is murdered at the climax of a private presentation of *Hamlet*, in which he plays Polonius. Inspector Appleby pursues some of the most famous names in the country, unearthing dreadful suspicion.

'Michael Innes is in a class by himself among writers of detective fiction' – *Times Literary Supplement*

THE LONG FAREWELL

Lewis Packford, the great Shakespearean scholar, was thought to have discovered a book annotated by the Bard – but there is no trace of this valuable object when Packford apparently commits suicide. Sir John Appleby finds a mixed bag of suspects at the dead man's house, who might all have a good motive for murder. The scholars and bibliophiles who were present might have been tempted by the precious document in Packford's possession. And Appleby discovers that Packford had two secret marriages, and that both of these women were at the house at the time of his death.

TITLES BY MICHAEL INNES AVAILABLE DIRECT
FROM HOUSE OF STRATUS

Quantity		£	$(US)	$(CAN)	€
	THE AMPERSAND PAPERS	6.99	12.95	19.95	13.50
	APPLEBY AND HONEYBATH	6.99	12.95	19.95	13.50
	APPLEBY AND THE OSPREYS	6.99	12.95	19.95	13.50
	APPLEBY AT ALLINGTON	6.99	12.95	19.95	13.50
	THE APPLEBY FILE	6.99	12.95	19.95	13.50
	APPLEBY ON ARARAT	6.99	12.95	19.95	13.50
	APPLEBY PLAYS CHICKEN	6.99	12.95	19.95	13.50
	APPLEBY TALKING	6.99	12.95	19.95	13.50
	APPLEBY TALKS AGAIN	6.99	12.95	19.95	13.50
	APPLEBY'S ANSWER	6.99	12.95	19.95	13.50
	APPLEBY'S END	6.99	12.95	19.95	13.50
	APPLEBY'S OTHER STORY	6.99	12.95	19.95	13.50
	AN AWKWARD LIE	6.99	12.95	19.95	13.50
	THE BLOODY WOOD	6.99	12.95	19.95	13.50
	CARSON'S CONSPIRACY	6.99	12.95	19.95	13.50
	A CHANGE OF HEIR	6.99	12.95	19.95	13.50
	CHRISTMAS AT CANDLESHOE	6.99	12.95	19.95	13.50
	A CONNOISSEUR'S CASE	6.99	12.95	19.95	13.50
	THE DAFFODIL AFFAIR	6.99	12.95	19.95	13.50
	DEATH AT THE CHASE	6.99	12.95	19.95	13.50
	DEATH AT THE PRESIDENT'S LODGING	6.99	12.95	19.95	13.50
	A FAMILY AFFAIR	6.99	12.95	19.95	13.50
	FROM LONDON FAR	6.99	12.95	19.95	13.50
	THE GAY PHOENIX	6.99	12.95	19.95	13.50

ALL HOUSE OF STRATUS BOOKS ARE AVAILABLE FROM GOOD BOOKSHOPS OR
DIRECT FROM THE PUBLISHER:

Internet: www.houseofstratus.com including synopses and features.

Email: sales@houseofstratus.com
info@houseofstratus.com
(please quote author, title and credit card details.)

TITLES BY MICHAEL INNES AVAILABLE DIRECT
FROM HOUSE OF STRATUS

Quantity		£	$(US)	$(CAN)	€
	Going It Alone	6.99	12.95	19.95	13.50
	Hamlet, Revenge!	6.99	12.95	19.95	13.50
	Hare Sitting Up	6.99	12.95	19.95	13.50
	Honeybath's Haven	6.99	12.95	19.95	13.50
	The Journeying Boy	6.99	12.95	19.95	13.50
	Lament For a Maker	6.99	12.95	19.95	13.50
	The Long Farewell	6.99	12.95	19.95	13.50
	The Man From the Sea	6.99	12.95	19.95	13.50
	Money From Holme	6.99	12.95	19.95	13.50
	The Mysterious Commission	6.99	12.95	19.95	13.50
	The New Sonia Wayward	6.99	12.95	19.95	13.50
	A Night of Errors	6.99	12.95	19.95	13.50
	Old Hall, New Hall	6.99	12.95	19.95	13.50
	The Open House	6.99	12.95	19.95	13.50
	Operation Pax	6.99	12.95	19.95	13.50
	A Private View	6.99	12.95	19.95	13.50
	The Secret Vanguard	6.99	12.95	19.95	13.50
	Sheiks and Adders	6.99	12.95	19.95	13.50
	Silence Observed	6.99	12.95	19.95	13.50
	Stop Press	6.99	12.95	19.95	13.50
	There Came Both Mist and Snow	6.99	12.95	19.95	13.50
	The Weight of the Evidence	6.99	12.95	19.95	13.50
	What Happened at Hazelwood	6.99	12.95	19.95	13.50

ALL HOUSE OF STRATUS BOOKS ARE AVAILABLE FROM GOOD BOOKSHOPS OR
DIRECT FROM THE PUBLISHER:

Tel:	Order Line 0800 169 1780 (UK) 800 724 1100 (USA) International +44 (0) 1845 527700 (UK) +01 845 463 1100 (USA)
Fax:	+44 (0) 1845 527711 (UK) +01 845 463 0018 (USA) (please quote author, title and credit card details.)
Send to:	House of Stratus Sales Department House of Stratus Inc. Thirsk Industrial Park 2 Neptune Road York Road, Thirsk Poughkeepsie North Yorkshire, YO7 3BX NY 12601 UK USA